KU-450-768

"Aaron, stop."

Her voice was breathy, aroused.

"Don't try to tell me you don't want me, Camille. I know you better than that."

"You don't know me at all."

What a load of crap she was feeding herself. He'd spent every moment of the past week memorizing her—from her body to the cadence of her speech, every sigh and every look. He'd lain awake each night listening to her breathe, drenching his senses with her. He knew Camille Fisher as well as he knew himself, better perhaps. "What have you convinced yourself of? What's going on in that sharp mind of yours?"

"I..."

As she searched for words, he cradled her foot, warming it.

"I don't want this between us."

He tipped her chin up until she looked into his eyes. "Baby, it's already between us."

The torment in her expression spoke of a battle raging within her. She knew he was right.

Seduction Under Fire

MELISSA CUTLER

MILLS & BOON

To my two beautiful kids, who cheer me every step of the way
while I chase down my dreams.

All the characters in this book have no existence outside
the imagination of the author, and have no relation
whatsoever to anyone bearing the same name or names.
They are not even distantly inspired by any individual
known or unknown to the author, and all the incidents
are pure invention.

All Rights Reserved including the right of reproduction
in whole or in part in any form. This edition is published
by arrangement with Harlequin Enterprises II BV/S.à.r.l.
The text of this publication or any part thereof may
not be reproduced or transmitted in any form or
by any means, electronic or mechanical, including
photocopying, recording, storage in an information
retrieval system, or otherwise, without the written
permission of the publisher.

® and TM are trademarks owned and used by the
trademark owner and/or its licensee. Trademarks marked
with ® are registered with the United Kingdom Patent
Office and/or the Office for Harmonisation in the
Internal Market and in other countries.

First published in Great Britain 2013
by Mills & Boon, an imprint of Harlequin (UK) Limited.
Large Print edition 2013
Harlequin (UK) Limited,
Eton House, 18-24 Paradise Road,
Richmond, Surrey TW9 1SR

© Melissa Cutler 2012

ISBN: 978 0 263 23807 5

Harlequin (UK) policy is to use papers that are natural,
renewable and recyclable products and made from
wood grown in sustainable forests. The logging
and manufacturing process conform to the legal
environmental regulations of the country of origin.

Printed and bound in Great Britain
by CPI Antony Rowe, Chippenham, Wiltshire

Dear Reader,

Luck is one of life's big mysteries. Some people believe we make our own luck, while others seem cursed with bad luck their whole lives. We all know people who seem to skate through life with golden tickets. Not that they don't earn their successes, but they seem flat-out luckier than the rest of us. One such person I know became the inspiration for the hero in *Seduction Under Fire*, park ranger Aaron Montgomery.

Aaron's life is one golden opportunity after another. He's on the fast track at work and, to top it all off, he's gorgeous (and knows it). Anything he's ever wanted, he's gotten… except the attention of his best friend's sister-in-law, Camille Fisher—and this ticks him off.

Camille is the unluckiest person she knows. All she ever wanted was to be a cop, but a freak accident has relegated her to a desk job—permanently. Nothing ever goes her way, and Aaron, with his golden goodness and perfect life, irritates her like salt in a wound. These two can't stand each other, but when they're targeted by a cartel, they're forced to rely on one another to survive. If they can find luck in love along the way, so much the better.

Happy reading!

Melissa Cutler

MELISSA CUTLER

is a flip-flop-wearing Southern California native living in San Diego with her husband, two children and a nervous Siamese cat. She spent her teenage years on the floor of her local bookstore's romance aisle making tough choices about which novels to buy with the measly paycheck from her filing-clerk job.

Her love for happily-ever-after stories continued into her job as a high school English teacher, and in 2008 she decided to take her romance-novel devotion to the next level by penning one herself. Halfway through that first book, she thought, *This is what I want to do every day for the rest of my life*, and she never looked back. She now divides her time between her dual writing passions—sexy small-town contemporaries and edge-of-your-seat romantic suspense.

Find out more about Melissa and her books at www.melissacutler.net. She loves to hear from readers, so drop her a line at cutlermail@yahoo.com. You can also find Melissa on Facebook and Twitter.

Chapter 1

Camille Fisher stood in a bathroom stall wearing the navy blue suit she'd picked out from a JCPenney clearance rack. The jacket buttoned across her chest, but it was a tight fit. With any luck, it would hold until after the press conference. She smoothed a hand down her skirt to make sure it covered her scar. It did, but she scowled at the streak of sweat her palm left on the polyester. Running too late to do anything more about the way she looked, she shielded her eyes from the mirror over the sink and reemerged into the bustling precinct.

Her boss caught up with her in the hallway,

wringing his hands. "Look, I know public speaking isn't your cup of tea, but I think it's a good move for you. Gets you out from behind your desk for a change."

Camille stopped short, reeling at the note of sympathy in his tone.

"I only agreed to this arrangement because a child's involved. I happen to enjoy working the dispatch desk." That was a whopper of a lie, but how dare Williamson pity her.

Five years ago, she was a force to be reckoned with, the youngest officer and only female ever promoted to the Special Forces unit in San Diego law enforcement history. As happened every time she thought about those days, the best six months of her life, she experienced a split second of exacting pain in her heart. Not a widespread pain like the bullet had been, but that of a needle. Worse than the pain, reflecting on her past left her feeling weak.

Above all else, Camille hated feeling weak.

"No need to get your back up, Fisher. We all appreciate you stepping up to the plate on this one. I'll see you out front in five."

Inside the lobby doors, Camille opened the three-day-old kidnapping file with trembling hands. She ran her fingertip around the edge of the glossy photo clipped to the front. If Williamson thought her involvement improved Rosalia Perez's chance of being recovered alive, then she owed it to the five-year-old smiling at her to do everything she could.

She pushed the double doors open and froze, stunned by the scene before her. The space between the San Diego Central Precinct and the surrounding high-rises was packed with spectators and journalists. The odor of hundreds of people standing in the midday sun swirled with the stench of car exhaust and city grime. Already on the verge of losing her breakfast, she gagged a little as she took her place in the line of law enforcement officers and government officials.

Camille didn't recognize the man dressed in civilian clothes who stepped to the podium. She tried to concentrate on his introduction of her, but she was working so hard to look confident that it took a nudge from Williamson for her to realize it was her turn to speak.

"Uh…I mean…welcome." She cringed. So much for a smooth beginning. The stares and expectations of the audience bore into her and she shuffled her notes, dumbstruck. Then she noticed Rosalia's photograph peeking out from behind some papers.

This one's for you, Rosalia.

With a deep breath, she squared her shoulders and began.

"At approximately eight o'clock on the morning of Tuesday, February 10, Rosalia Perez boarded a school bus to Balboa Elementary. When class started at eight-thirty, she was marked absent by her teacher. Following the school's unverified absence protocol, a phone call was placed to her home at eight-forty-five and was answered by Rosalia's maternal grandmother, who is a non-English speaker. An interpreter at the school was summoned and a second phone call was placed at nine o'clock, during which the grandmother said that Rosalia had ridden the bus.

"The school bus driver confirmed that his bus dropped Rosalia off in front of Balboa Elementary at eight-ten. By nine-thirty, the girl's mother, Maria Delgado, had arrived at the school. She, along with the school secretary, contacted the police to report her daughter missing. An Amber Alert was issued at nine-forty-five.

"Rosalia Perez is five years old, weighs fifty-one pounds and stands forty-four inches—or just under four feet—tall. She has shoulder-length brown hair and a strawberry-colored birthmark on her forehead above her left eyebrow. You'll find a photograph of her in your press packet.

"Interviews conducted with adults present on the Balboa Elementary campus that morning yielded no information regarding Rosalia's disappearance, but two student eyewitnesses report seeing Rosalia, before school, approach a brown two-door sedan driven by a dark-haired man.

"At this time, our main suspect is Rosalia's biological father, Rodrigo Perez, aka El Ocho, a member of the crime organization in Mexico commonly known as the Cortez Cartel. He is suspected of being in the United States illegally. He is approximately five feet eight inches tall with light brown skin and short, black hair. In every photograph we've acquired, he's wearing black leather gloves. He is considered armed and extremely dangerous.

"I will be conducting briefings at twelve o'clock each day in the main conference room of this precinct to keep the public as informed as our investigation allows." She glanced around for the man who had introduced her. "Am I taking questions?"

He nodded and the entire throng of reporters stood at once, shouting.

Camille gestured to a woman wearing a red suit in the front row.

"How can the police be sure Rosalia hasn't been taken to Mexico by her father?"

"The Border Patrol is immediately notified of

all Amber Alerts, but with the nearly two-hour gap between the time Rosalia was last seen and when she was reported missing, we have no way of knowing whether she was taken out of the country, especially since the abduction site is only twenty minutes north of the Mexican border. We are working to gain permission from the Mexican government to widen our search to include Baja."

Camille took a dozen more questions before gathering her notes and giving the podium over to the man who introduced her. Trembling with adrenaline, she nodded to her boss and walked past the line of officials and back through the double doors.

The relative silence of the precinct was a relief. Mostly, she couldn't wait to change out of her suit. From the chair at her desk she grabbed her duffel bag and heard her cell phone ringing in her purse.

When she saw the text message, she smiled and snagged Williamson as he walked by. "I just got word my sister's in labor. I'll be back at work tomorrow in time for the press briefing."

"Congratulations to your family. And give your dad my best. Remind him I still owe him for the burger he bought me last month."

Camille's father was retired, but his years on the force were legendary. She was constantly asked by her superiors to give her father their regards or forced to sit patiently through retellings of his most heroic moments. There had been a time Camille dreamed of following in his footsteps. The familiar needle of pain pierced her heart, but she refused to dwell. No more thoughts of dying dreams, not when she was about to become an aunt.

Juliana was two years Camille's junior and as different from her as a sister could be. A lifetime of strained relations had finally given way to friendship two years ago, after Juliana fell in love with Camille's former partner, Jacob. That he was the man responsible for Camille's accidental shooting was immaterial. She'd known the risks of her high-stakes job when she signed on.

She grabbed her duffel and kept moving. She'd

change out of the uncomfortable skirt and flats after she checked in with her sister.

Aaron Montgomery's eyeballs hurt.

He could barely see the sun through the heavily tinted windows of the meeting room, yet it was still painful. Not even his special hangover energy drink helped when his head ached this badly. Sure he'd wanted to celebrate Tuesday's big arrests, but what in God's name made him down those last three tequila shots instead of calling it a night?

The answer, of course, was a petite college senior—at least, that's what he thought she said—with long chocolate-colored hair and a waistline so tiny that when she ground against him on the dance floor, her little black skirt kept sliding down to reveal her thong.

Ah, good times.

"Something funny, Montgomery?" barked Thomas Dreyer, the ICE Field Office Director, who stood at the head of the table.

Aaron mashed his lips together in an effort to

stop smiling. "Just thinking about how those cartel runners almost crapped their pants when we caught them, sir."

"Add those two to the ten we expedited in December and we're starting to send a clear message that these lowlifes can't move guns through our country's deserts and get away with it. If the cartels want to wage war against each other in Mexico, I'll be damned if they're going to do it with American firepower."

"I couldn't agree with you more, sir." Staying on Dreyer's good side was proving to be a tricky act—the man had no sense of humor—but Aaron was an expert at being a team player. And this was a team he was determined to rise to the top of.

As was usually the case in his life, Aaron had been handed the opportunity. His best friend, Jacob, referred to his luck as Aaron's Golden Ticket. The label was fine for a joke, but Aaron knew better. He didn't wait for luck to strike him where he stood, but instead kept his eyes open, ready to move into the path of the bolt at the first sign of a spark. So when, a year ago, the Federal Immigration and Customs Enforcement agency, better known as ICE, handpicked him to participate in a regional joint task force to combat drug, guns and human trafficking through the Southern California desert, Aaron seized the opportunity.

And he had a goal for himself. A big one.

He had no interest in being a boss man, standing at the head of the table as an administrator like Dreyer. His ultimate goal was to prove his worth as an ICE field agent. Maybe undercover. Definitely abroad.

As one of two Park Rangers on a unit comprised primarily of Border Patrol officers and ICE intelligence agents, Aaron was in ambitious company. Although he came to the unit with thirteen years' experience as a Backcountry Park Ranger, he'd invested months of rigorous field training in weaponry and combat tactics and countless hours of classroom time to understand border policing laws so when the opportunity to transfer from

Park Ranger to ICE agent presented itself, he'd be ready.

The challenge couldn't have come at a better time. The diversions that used to satisfy his wanderlust had lost their flavor. Though he still thought his Mustang Shelby GT 500 was the best money he'd ever spent, he no longer took it for day trips simply for the thrill of the drive. Even the club scenes he frequented felt like a waste of time. Rock climbing, speedboating, skydiving—nothing he tried could take away the restless dissatisfaction that had settled into his bones.

Last night, he'd stayed out way too late with Little Miss Thong because she was exactly the type of girl that got his blood pumping. But sometime during the night, the pointlessness of what he was doing dawned on him. Time and youth were slipping away from him at an alarming rate, a revelation he counteracted by drinking and dancing more than usual.

Since Jacob's wedding a year and a half ago, Aaron felt *off*.

At first, he thought it was because Jacob no longer had much time to spend with him, but it was more than that. Maybe he was subconsciously jealous of Jacob's marital bliss or maybe Aaron was bored, but the discontent that had dogged him since his friend's wedding was damned annoying.

"As I was saying," Dreyer said with a hard glance at Aaron, "the latest intel is that the Cortez Cartel's weapons distribution operation is being headquartered near the Baja capital city of La Paz, along the Sea of Cortez." He pushed a button on his laptop and a satellite image of the Baja peninsula projected onto the wall behind him.

"As we already suspected, the Mexican government's crackdown on cartels within Baja's border cities has spurred them to move to obscure locations and utilize more creative means to smuggle weapons into their country."

With another push of a button, Dreyer projected a grainy photo of a Hispanic man with jet-black hair and a round, oily face. "This is our next target, Rodrigo Perez, Alejandro Milán's second-in-command. Perez has been running the weapons-smuggling division of the Cortez Cartel for approximately one year and manages a crew of at least thirty men."

Aaron felt the vibration of his cell phone in his shirt pocket. He flipped it open to find a short text message—*Jul n labr.*

"Look at that," he muttered to himself. "I'm about to be a godfather."

He caught the eye of Nicholas Wells, the other Park Ranger in the unit, and held up his phone. "Family emergency," he mouthed, scooting out of his chair. He opened the door and slipped into the bright afternoon, his headache forgotten.

She should have known he'd be at the birth of Juliana and Jacob's child—he was her brother-in-law's best friend, after all—but Camille's stomach still lurched when she heard the deafening rumble of Aaron's obnoxious car pull into the hospital parking garage behind her.

Unwilling to park on the same level as him, she

drove past whole rows of available parking spots, waiting for him to choose one first. To her chagrin, he passed every open spot, too. In her rearview mirror, she saw Aaron chuckling behind his wraparound sunglasses and knew he was onto her plan. Even in the dim light of the garage, his dimples sparkled. The man was like a barbed thorn in her side—irritating and impossible to dislodge.

Finally he conceded and pulled into a space on the fourth level. Camille drove to the roof.

Then it occurred to her that in a matter of minutes, she'd be sitting in a waiting room with the man she'd successfully avoided for over a year. She thunked her forehead on the steering wheel and groaned.

She first met Jacob's best friend two years earlier, and it had been a miserable experience. Simply put, Aaron was the most arrogant man she'd ever known. Handsome to a fault, with wavy blond hair and a body so meticulously ripped it was the perfect advertisement for his bloated ego, he'd made her feel like a piece of meat from the moment he introduced himself without raising his eyes higher than her chest.

When he figured out she wasn't going to drool all over his showy muscles, lame jokes and expensive car, he'd been equally put off by her.

At Juliana and Jacob's wedding, Camille put on her game face and tolerated Aaron for the single dance required of the maid of honor and best man, then spent the rest of the reception watching him hit on all the young, single women in attendance. She couldn't believe how easily they fell for his boyish good looks and perfect body. They didn't even notice he was treating them like interchangeable objects. She made a game of predicting which one he'd invite to his room that night. Because the wedding party had rooms on the same hotel floor, it was an easy mystery to solve.

And her prediction had been correct.

She knew Aaron thought she was a killjoy, but unlike the girls falling all over him at Juliana's wedding, Camille didn't require the validation of a man. And it was a good thing, too, because being a young female cop with a statuesque figure was like being an island in a sea of chauvinism. Why this particular chauvinist rubbed her the wrong way, Camille wasn't sure. Frankly, she tried not to think about it—ever.

She grabbed her bag of clothes and purse and locked her car. When she got to the stairwell, she paused. Which would Aaron be less likely to take—the stairs or the elevator? She decided to take the stairs, even though her dressy shoes were beginning to rub, because it would preclude any chance of being stuck in the tight confines of an elevator with him. If he chose the stairs, she could hang back and let him go first.

As she turned the corner onto the fourth level landing, Aaron materialized in the stairwell.

"Camille, what a…pleasant surprise," he dead-panned, falling into step beside her.

"I see you're still compensating for your short-comings with that offensive car."

He chortled. "It's good to know time hasn't soft-ened your icy heart."

Narrowing her eyes, Camille picked up the pace. So much for hanging behind; she wouldn't give him the satisfaction. She motioned to his dark glasses. "Are you hungover again? Funny how every time I see you, you've been drinking too much. Maybe I'll send you an AA pamphlet."

With her skirt and shoes slowing her down, Aaron paced her effortlessly.

"Gee," he said, "that's a nice suit you're wearing. Borrowing your grandma's clothes again, are you?"

"You're such a pig."

"And you're still a shrew, so we're even."

That was enough for Camille. "Out of my way," she snarled. Elbowing him in the chest, she propelled herself into the lead.

He quickened his steps to match hers. "Always such a bully. When're you going to figure out no one likes a bully, Blondie?"

"When're you going to figure out I hate you, you misogynist prick?"

"Sweetheart, I figured that out the day we met,

and I dropped to my knees, thanking the Lord for small favors."

They broke into a sprint, their feet flying and their knees pumping like football players running a high-step drill. Camille knew she was acting immature, but she simply had to be the first person to the bottom of the stairs, the first person through the hospital doors, the first one to reach Juliana's bedside.

As they traversed the last flight of stairs, Aaron shouldered past her, taking the steps two at a time. When Camille tried to match his stride, one of her shoes flew off. She grabbed the railing to keep from pitching headfirst to the ground.

Aaron reached the bottom level of the parking garage and scooped up Camille's shoe. He turned to face her with a smug smile. "I'm sure your grandmother will want this back."

Gasping at the insult, she yanked her other shoe off and hurled it at him.

He ducked, but his laughter was drowned out

by a revving engine, its echo thunderous in the confines of the garage.

A white minivan screeched to a halt behind Aaron as its side door opened. Two masked men armed with fully automatic assault rifles were staged inside. Aaron whipped his head around, but it was too late. The men pulled him in and pointed their guns at Camille.

"In the van, *puta*. Now!" one of the men shouted at her.

Impossible. This couldn't be happening. She was there for the birth of her niece.

"Camille, run," Aaron called from within the van.

Run? Where? The only route was back up the stairs and then she'd still be trapped in the garage. Her eyes settled on the rifles, AK-47 knockoffs, probably Romanian. Wherever they were from, the guns made her only choice perfectly clear. Numbly, she got into the van.

Aaron sagged against the floor with half-closed eyelids as though he were drifting to sleep. "Aaron, what...? Why are you—" She yelped, turning toward the pain in her upper arm. An unmasked, baby-faced man with slicked-back hair was plunging a needle into her.

"Oh, God, no." Then her tongue, along with the rest of her body, grew heavy, and she crumpled over Aaron's limp form.

Chapter 2

Body odor. Not the occasional whiff of someone who forgot to apply deodorant, but the cloying, inescapable stench of people who, as a habit, did not bathe. The smell was so pungent, Aaron tasted it in his mouth as it hung open, slack and drooling due to the drug he'd been injected with.

Time passed indeterminately. Perhaps they drove for an hour, maybe longer. He couldn't see anything except the booted feet of his captors, nor feel anything except the weight of Camille sprawled over him. No one spoke except for comments in Spanish said in whispers too soft for

Aaron to translate, though he was adept at the language.

When the van stopped moving, the kidnappers stirred.

"Ustedes dos llévense al hombre." You two take the man. *"Cuidado, Perez lo quiere ileso."* Careful, Perez wants him unharmed.

Rodrigo Perez.

With the mention of that name, Aaron knew why he'd been taken and what they were going to do to him. As the man who arrested two of Perez's operatives, Aaron was going to help the cartel send a message to the U.S. government. Today he was going to die. Probably beheaded. Most likely paraded around the streets of Tijuana on a stick. And Camille, poor unlucky Camille, was going to die, too.

He was dragged from the van to a small plane on a cracked blacktop runway in the middle of a lettuce field. Camille was slung over the shoulder of a short man, her legs dangling and her skirt bunched, revealing the white of her panties. Another man walked to her, chuckling, and pulled her skirt higher.

Realization of his powerlessness crashed over Aaron. These men could do whatever they wanted to Camille—rape, kill, anything—and Aaron couldn't protect her. It was one thing to die as a result of his dangerous job. It was something much worse to watch another suffer, particularly a woman, for no reason other than her close proximity to trouble when it struck.

He was shoved through a side door in the plane and dumped on the floor. Camille was dropped at his side. With much effort, he turned his head to see her. Her eyes were not glazed over from the drug, nor did she look afraid at all, which threw Aaron off. He'd been prepared to console her. Instead she met his look with a sharp, confident gaze, as though she was trying to give *him* courage.

The plane taxied, then angled into the air. Aaron shifted until the back of his arm touched Camille's hand. She wiggled her fingers against his skin.

Of all the people in the world to be the last each saw before dying, that they were stuck with each other was definitive proof that God had an ironic sense of humor.

When the plane reached cruising altitude, some-one moved between Camille's legs. Aaron could tuck his chin enough to see the man's slim form, but not what he was doing. He had a pretty good idea, though. Against the back of his hand, he felt her skirt being raised. Someone Aaron couldn't see laughed and whooped. Aaron took Camille's hand firmly in his and looked into her eyes. For the first time, she seemed afraid.

Don't think about it, Camille. Look at me and turn your mind off.

After a minute, her look of fear evolved into confusion. The man above Camille smacked Aar-on's hand away and rolled her to her stomach. Then Aaron saw the harness.

Black straps looped around her thighs and shoulders, meeting in a rectangle of material against her back with attachments for the master jumper. Camille was being fitted with skydiving gear, the kind used in tandem jumps. When her harness was on, the man left her on her stomach. She turned to Aaron, her expression questioning. Aaron tried to speak, but his words came out distorted beyond understanding.

The same man moved over Aaron, lifting his legs and putting his tandem harness in place. Aaron had enough experience and skill to be a solo jumper, but like most people, he'd started with tandem jumping, where the novice is strapped to the front of an experienced jumper—the one with the parachute.

Aaron's master jumper began the process of binding them together. Aaron had read reports of instances where this hadn't been done correctly and the results were as gruesome as one might imagine. Hopefully these guys knew what they were doing.

The door of the plane opened and the howl of air moving at a hundred miles per hour eclipsed all other sounds in the cabin. The kidnappers heaved two wooden crates fitted with chutes through the opening. Too bad Aaron would never have the chance to tell his team about the Cortez Cartel's method for smuggling weapons into Mexico.

Goggles were put on Camille and Aaron, which seemed like an odd bit of caring for hostage-taking narco-terrorists, and they were hauled to standing on weak but functioning legs. With the press of the master jumper's belly nudging him, Aaron dragged his heavy feet toward the open door. He remembered how intimidating that opening, with the scream of the wind, looked on his first jump, and turned, seeking Camille to bolster her courage.

She stood behind Aaron, lining up for her jump. Though he was pretty sure she'd never been sky-diving before, he shouldn't have been surprised by the look of steely determination on her face. She might be the most grating woman he'd ever met, but he had to admire her fortitude. Camille was one tough broad.

She dipped her head in a terse nod, then shrank

away with the rest of the plane as Aaron fell into the infinite blue horizon.

Camille's heart pounded in her ears as she fell to earth. The fear of not knowing if the chute would open or if her harness would hold overrode all other thought during the free fall that seemed to last an eternity. Finally, the force of the unfurling chute jolted her back. Cold air whipped at her bare legs and feet. She was probably the first woman in history to skydive in a business suit, which was an honor she could have done without—and a perfect example of her rotten luck.

Camille used to believe she had fantastic luck. Five years ago, while lying in a hospital bed, she felt lucky to have cheated death, lucky that when Jacob misfired his gun, the bullet ripped through her thigh and not her head or an artery. In the days following the shooting, she felt lucky to keep the leg with the promise of walking again.

But as weeks and months passed, luck abandoned her. Oh, she could walk—for a little while before the throbbing pain became unbearable. And she could run—for a minute or two at a time. Soon, her recovery stalled.

What crushed her the most was the damage to her right hand, even though the bullet hadn't come close to it. No matter how diligently she worked in rehab, her right hand shook uncontrollably when she held a gun. She discovered that little nugget of joy four weeks after the accident, her first time back at the firing range. She tried to load the magazine of her Glock 23 and her hand shook like there was an earthquake inside her body. She couldn't even get a round off.

Her mandatory, department-issued therapist called it post-traumatic stress disorder. That sounded pretty official and all, but giving a name to her problem didn't magically fix her.

Nothing could fix her.

Just like that, Camille's temporary assignment to the dispatch desk took on the horrible stench of permanency. Her family encouraged her to pick a different career—if she ever heard the saying

When one door closes, another opens again, she'd hang herself—but being a top-rate police officer was all she'd ever wanted. It was her one thing, her only thing.

She knew why she'd been kidnapped. Her image was splashed on the news naming Rosalia Perez's father as a suspect, and a few hours later she was snatched by a group of Spanish-speaking thugs with the financial resources to own a private plane and an arsenal of assault weapons.

Her remorse was solely for Aaron, whose only offense was arriving at the hospital at the same time she did. At least he had the good fortune to be taken hostage with a former Special Forces officer. If even the smallest opportunity for escape opened, Camille would try to get Aaron to safety. She might hate the guy, but no one deserved to die this way. She had a vague recollection of Jacob gushing about Aaron's assignment as a Park Ranger to an ICE task force, but she had no idea if he possessed skills that could aid their escape. The only Park Rangers she'd ever met had been a pair of granola-eating trail guides.

During the five-minute descent, she focused on determining their location. The ocean sat to the east and a long range of foothills sprawled over the west and south. What really struck her about the landscape was its desolation.

Save for a large city to the south along the shoreline and a highway running north and south, there wasn't much to see. No suburban developments and few signs of life. The ground, from the shoreline to the tops of the foothills, was blanketed with rocks, tall-reaching cacti and scruffy desert plants. This had to be Mexico. Nowhere in America would such a large stretch of land abutting the ocean be free of people.

Before Camille touched down, she saw they were met by six mangy horses, one of which had a rider, a stout middle-aged Latino man with a thick mustache and a wavy shock of black hair. Two horses were strapped to a wagon laden with the wooden crates. The remaining horses were riderless and saddled.

She landed hard and grunted in pain when her knees hit gravel. The jumper attached to her toppled over her and shouted something in Spanish, then detached their harnesses and hauled her to her feet. Aaron stood nearby, a rifle pressed to his back. Despite it being February, the desert sun blazed against Camille's fair skin. She licked her dry, cracked lips and tried unsuccessfully to swallow.

When someone shoved her toward him, her jelly legs lurched and she tripped over a rock. She would have fallen except Aaron reached out and caught her. With an expressionless face, he pulled her to his side and maintained a steadying hand on her elbow.

Mr. Mustache gestured to a chestnut-colored horse. With tentative steps, Camille approached it. She wiggled a foot into the stirrup and tried to hoist herself on, but her muscles refused to comply.

Aaron's hands encircled her waist. "I've got you," he whispered.

As he lifted, Camille hefted her leg over the saddle. Aaron swung behind her. It was the closest she'd been to a man in a long, long time. Check that—ever. She squirmed, desperate to put an inch or two between them.

"Easy there," he muttered. To Camille's mortification, he grabbed her hips and pulled her onto his groin. "Sorry." His breath on her skin sent an involuntary shudder through her spine. "This saddle's too small for the both of us."

No kidding. "Just keep your hands to yourself."

He responded with a quiet snort. "We're going to die, Camille, and even if we weren't, you're not my type."

"Believe me when I say that's a relief."

With Mr. Mustache holding the reins of Camille and Aaron's horse, the caravan began a slow trot into the foothills, away from the city she'd seen in the distance.

As they rode in silence over an endless expanse

of shrubs and sand, Camille caught a whiff of Aaron's scent for the first time—clean, like freshly laundered cotton. Discreetly, she turned her face toward his neck and inhaled. No doubt about it, despite their ordeal, the man smelled like laundry straight out of the dryer. She squeezed her arms down, certain she didn't smell as nice.

She'd learned the hard way that when men were as good-looking as Aaron, they were used to getting whatever they wanted. Aaron, in particular, oozed entitlement from his every pore. As though being born beautiful was anything more than lucky genes.

It irritated Camille to be the foil to his physical perfection. She neither looked nor smelled as good as he did. She felt awkward and unnatural on the horse while he was graceful and practiced. It was not an exaggeration to say he made being taken hostage look elegant and easy. No wonder she'd avoided him the past two years. His very existence felt toxic to her own.

When the trail turned steeply upward, Camille

was forced to lean into his chest. He tensed in response. She turned to find him scowling.

"Don't worry," she growled, "it's not a come-on. You're not my type either."

Not that it mattered in these last few minutes of his life, but no way would Aaron embarrass himself by sporting an erection while sharing a saddle with Camille Fisher. There would be no masking it since she was sitting on his lap, a position only slightly more comfortable than enduring the constant wiggling of her derriere.

Somehow, he had to figure out a way to stop his body's reaction. First, he needed to quit smelling her hair, which was difficult because it was the most exquisite head of hair he'd ever seen, hanging in thick tresses down her back, inches from his nose. As the trail turned steep, Camille reclined into him and it took all his mental wrangling to not bury his face in it.

The second key to his success was not looking at or touching her long, perfectly toned legs to see if her skin was as soft as it looked. He remembered those legs from Jacob and Juliana's wedding, how they looked holding up her red dress. What a waste, he'd thought at the time, to give such a body to a foul-tempered harpy.

The moment they crested a hill and a compound came into view, nestled in a narrow valley, Aaron began searching for a weakness in the layout he could exploit as an escape route. If there was one, though, he couldn't find it. The towering cinder-block wall surrounding three squat, houselike buildings was topped with thick ropes of barbed wire. The iron-barred entrance gate on the east side, currently guarded by two men with rifles, was the only break in the wall.

The horses were led to the south of the compound, under a lean-to that served as a stable, where a pudgy man with wide-set eyes and a long, thin mouth like a frog took the reins. Aaron hadn't seen a single car yet, which meant they would have to flee on horseback. With that in mind, he made damn sure he knew where the tack and saddles were stored before he and Camille were dragged from the horse and marched toward the entrance gate.

Barefoot, Camille stumbled along the inhospitable desert terrain. Aaron kept a firm hand on her elbow, steering her around the worst of the rocks and prickly cacti blanketing the ground, but her lack of footwear was one more strike against the probability of a successful escape, as if the odds weren't impossible already.

By the time they reached the courtyard created by the buildings' U-shaped layout, his hope for freedom had evaporated. The barbed wire-topped fence looked even more ominous up close and, with every step he took over the bullet-casing-littered ground, he counted another man and even more guns. They didn't stand a chance of escaping this place with their lives.

They were prodded past an unmarked white delivery truck and a table loaded with what looked like satellite communication equipment and into the largest building that seemed to serve as the living quarters. Halfway down a dim hallway, they were muscled into a room that was empty save for the rusty metal chair Aaron was shoved into.

With a half dozen armed men surrounding him and a gun nudging Camille's back, he didn't put up a fight. Not even when a man with heavy acne scarring, holding a white rope, stepped forward to bind his hands behind the seatback and his legs to the legs of the chair. Within minutes, a second chair appeared and Camille was similarly bound.

Aaron met her gaze. The toughness he'd come to admire was still there, but shadowed by a hint of fear. As if maybe she'd done her own assessment of their odds and found them as bleak as he had.

From behind the cluster of men, a little girl with round, fearful eyes shuffled forward.

A tall, wiry man knelt next to her, whispering. She looked as though she was ready to run, but the man gripped her soiled red shirt tightly. She looked at Aaron and two tears rolled down her cheeks.

With a push from the man, she spoke in a mousy whisper in English. "We will send your picture to the American government." After more prompting in Spanish, she continued. "Your government has one day to free the prisoners you took this week." She paused and shook her head as more tears fell.

The man grabbed her frizzy black hair and shook her hard. *"Habla ahora o no comerás esta noche."* Say it right now or you will not eat tonight.

For the first time in his life, Aaron wanted to hurt another human being. His nostrils flared as he struggled for self-control.

"Or...or..." the girl continued softly, "you will die."

A man stepped forward with a camera and clicked twice. Aaron was certain he was captured in the picture displaying a sneer that matched the rage he felt. He wanted to shout at these men for defiling the girl's innocence, but it would be stupid to reveal his understanding of their language. So he held his tongue as the man dragged the girl from the room. The rest of the crowd filed out and multiple locks clicked into place.

The atmosphere was heavy after the men left, punctuated only by the sound of Aaron's labored, anger-fueled breathing.

"I know that girl," Camille said, staring vacantly at the door. "That was Rosalia Perez."

Chapter 3

Camille was looking for a flaw in their captors' plan, an opening in their defense—anything to take advantage of. Now that the drug had worn off and her mind and body could work in harmony, she began to think in earnest about escaping.

Almost a perfect square, the room showed little promise for their freedom. Though it had two doors, the one they'd entered through and another that opened to the courtyard, judging from the barred window adjacent to it, she felt safe in assuming both were locked. The concrete floor was barren except for their chairs. Not even a nail hung from the cracked cinder-block walls. No electrical outlets, no lights—nothing.

She squirmed, testing the knots, and felt a stinging pain in the side of her right hand. She groped with her fingers and found the source, a sharp barb where the rusty metal of the chair had eroded. That, she could work with.

Aaron's voice cut through the silence. "I'm sorry I got you into this mess."

Camille blinked. "*I'm* the one to blame. Whatever prisoners they want released, they must think I'm a good pawn since I went on national news today implicating Rodrigo Perez in the kidnapping of his daughter. He's a major player in the—"

"I know who he is. He's the next target of my task force because he's running weapons through the desert. I'm the one who arrested the prisoners they want released."

"Oh." She pulled her face back, shock rendering her momentarily speechless. "Jacob said you'd joined a task force, but I didn't know you had the authority to make arrests."

"What did you think I do for a living?"

"You're a Park Ranger. I figured you were cat-aloging cacti and leading hikes. How was I to know you were in the field hunting international fugitives?"

Aaron huffed. "You had no idea Park Rangers are fully sworn-in peace officers, same as you?"

"Er, nope." *And you can shut up about how ignorant I am, Mr. Perfect.*

"I'm sorry to burst your bubble, but you don't get to take credit for getting us killed."

She wiggled the rope. "Hey, we're not dead yet. You can only take credit for getting us kidnapped."

"We're tied up in a barbed wire-rimmed compound in the middle of the Mexican desert, surrounded by men with assault rifles and God knows what else, without any money or transportation. Excuse me for not feeling very optimistic."

Camille shrugged noncommittally. "Any idea where we are?"

"The Cortez Cartel has a stronghold in La Paz.

Given the orientation of the water and the sparseness of the population, that's my best guess."

"I've never heard of La Paz."

"It's not very touristy, not like Cabo. ICE thinks the cartel works it like a mafia, with their fingerprints everywhere, even in the local police."

"Is the Cortez Cartel Mexico's most powerful?"

"Not by a long shot. That would be the La Mérida Cartel. Before he was arrested, their leader, Gael Vega, started his own militia that rivals the Mexican military in power."

They were warned of their captors' return by the sound of boots in the hall followed by clicking locks moments before the door opened. The man who had taken their horses entered holding a bottle of brownish water and a bowl of rice, followed by an armed guard who stopped in the doorway.

He held the water to Camille's lips. She turned away, not about to let it pollute her body. The man chased her mouth with the bottle and nudged at her closed lips a few times. Poking her with a spoonful of rice, he shouted in Spanish and gestured to the window. When she didn't relent, he moved to Aaron, who also refused. Only two minutes after arriving, the man and his guard left.

"Wish I'd paid more attention in my high school Spanish classes," she grumbled.

"He said this is your last chance for food until he returns tomorrow morning. And that you would be stupid to refuse."

Of course the Golden Boy spoke fluent Spanish. But she had to admit, the skill might come in handy when they escaped. And they would escape, she thought as she wiggled her wrists, teasing the rope against the barb.

Hours later, long after the room had gone dark and Aaron was only an outline as he sat in silence a few feet away, Camille felt the rope finally give. Her hands bore the evidence of her effort with countless scrapes and puncture wounds from the rusty barb. Thank goodness she kept up with her tetanus shot.

Once free, she bent to work on the ropes binding her feet.

"What the…?" Aaron said.

"Those idiots shouldn't have used such old chairs. Mine had a sharp edge perfect for sawing rope."

"Good thing, too, because the clock's ticking, Blondie. We don't have time—"

Camille's first order of business as an escapee was to make one minor but vital point with Aaron. "Let's get something straight—don't ever call me Blondie again. Or *Sweetie* or *Doll* or any of those derogatory nicknames you're so fond of. I hate it. Understood?"

"Okay, I got it."

Satisfied, Camille began untying the rope around Aaron's wrists.

"Like I was saying," he continued, "we don't have much time before frog man and his bodyguard bring us breakfast at gunpoint."

Camille looked out the window at the first glow of predawn. If they were lucky, they had maybe an hour or two to devise a plan. "As far as weapons go, we've got this rope and these chairs, but that's not enough. I've got another idea, but it'll take some time to prep."

"Care to explain?"

"Not yet." What she had in mind would open her up to all kinds of ridicule, so she decided to keep mum until she was certain it would work. While Aaron freed his legs from the chair, Camille slipped to the darkest corner of the room and took off her bra.

Aaron's heart pounded so loudly, he was surprised Camille couldn't hear it. Without weapons to defend themselves, they were as good as dead. And what weapon could they find in this room that would be any match for automatic rifles?

The chairs were too ungainly. The guard would have plenty of time to react if he saw a twenty-pound metal chair coming at him. He tested the individual spokes and chair legs, hoping to break one off and use it as a club or knife, but no such luck. He could wield a shard of glass from the window, but if anyone were in the courtyard, they would hear it break.

"Camille, I'm running out of ideas." He glanced in her direction.

What he saw was so at odds with what he expected that words died in his throat. Trying to ignore the taut points of her nipples beneath her thin white camisole, he watched her bite a hole in the beige bra she held.

"You got a weapon stashed in there or something?"

She ignored him and pulled a long, thin wire from inside the bra cup, then snapped it in half. "Bet you didn't know underwire is flat like a screwdriver."

"No, can't say I've thought much about bras except how to get them off as quickly as possible."

Rolling her eyes, she turned away and put her bra on. Still confused, Aaron gaped at her back. Once she'd righted her clothes, she knelt before the door that led outside. Using the blunt end of the underwire, she loosened the doorknob's screws.

"Throwing a doorknob at them is better than nothing, but hardly game changing, MacGyver."

She glanced sideways at him. "You're a dense man. We've been over this already. I hate nicknames. Take off one of your socks so we can put the doorknob in it. We can do serious damage to someone's head that way."

Aaron grinned, genuinely impressed. Even so, he couldn't stem the urge to tease her. "I didn't think a chick would be so handy to have around."

She jumped to her feet and rushed him. With fiery eyes, she poked him hard in the chest and waved the underwire beneath his nose. "You ought to show more respect to the person who's saving your life." She poked him again. "I'm not one of those helpless cupcakes you waste your time with. I graduated head of my class at the police academy and was the first female Special Forces Officer in San Diego. Those sons of bitches have no idea what a mistake they made messing with me."

Aaron held up his hands in surrender. The gesture lost significance by the fact that he was chuckling. For some sick and twisted reason he didn't care to analyze, he liked her when she was all riled up this way. "Cupcakes?"

Camille snorted and went back to work on the doorknob screws. "Yeah, well, that's what they look like to me with their poofy hair and fake nails and fluffy clothes—little pink frosted cupcakes with sprinkles. Completely free of substance."

Aaron gawked at her. Not for the first time since their ordeal began, she'd rendered him speechless.

She was right. Most of the women he knew were a bunch of cupcakes compared to her, a woman so self-sufficient and physically capable that she was the one planning to save *his* life. She was the one fashioning tools out of her bra and improvising weaponry. He supposed he hadn't noticed sooner because they'd never been in a clinch situation before, but the lady was a badass.

He was fascinated…and irritated as hell to realize it.

Well, he had no intention of standing around and letting Camille be the only hero. While she finessed the external doorknob to stay in place, he removed his sock, slid the interior knob inside and took a few practice swings. As far as bludgeons went, this one would do nicely.

"The guard'll have a gun, so the trick will be to catch him unaware," he deliberated.

Camille stood and adjusted her skirt. "I thought of that, too. That's where our rope will come in handy."

Their animosity forgotten, they scooted their chairs together and hashed out a plan. Stripped of sarcasm and defensiveness, Aaron was surprised by how similarly their minds worked. Within minutes, they knew how to proceed and the role each would play.

They took positions on either side of the hallway door and waited. Feeling more confident than he had since being taken hostage, he smiled at Camille, who responded with a sly grin of her own.

In the two years he'd known her, this was the first time he'd ever seen her smile. He liked the effect it had on her features. It didn't soften her but made her look more powerful and capable and all those things Aaron was discovering this extraordinary woman was beneath her cold exterior. He studied her, mesmerized by her complexity, as she stood with a rope in hand, ready to spring at her enemy.

They had plenty of warning when it was showtime. Boots in the hallway, a lock rattling. With the click of the second lock, Aaron's muscles tensed. Camille crouched, leaning toward the door, the rope tight in her hands.

This was going to be fast.

The whole choreographed sequence would take less than a minute. The placement of their footfalls and the timing of their moves had to be exact. He and Camille would have to work as though they were breathing in unison.

The door swung wide, hiding Aaron behind it. Holding his position, he gripped the bludgeon and prayed.

* * *

Camille let the man get both feet in the room and register that the chairs were empty. She dropped the rope over his head and pulled him against her, strangling him as she moved backward three steps.

The guard played his part perfectly. He ran into the room and faced Camille and her hostage, his finger on the trigger of his rifle, shouting at her in Spanish.

"In," Camille said.

At her cue, Aaron kicked the door closed. With unflinching purpose, he brought the bludgeon down on the guard's head, felling him instantly. Then, working in perfect synchronization, Aaron straddled the guard and swung the bludgeon as Camille pushed her captive toward him. It took two thumps with the doorknob before he crumpled atop the unconscious guard.

Aaron stood over the two fallen bodies looking the part of a victorious warrior, surveying his conquered foes. Camille tried to be subtle about it, but she couldn't take her eyes off him. He gripped the bludgeon in his hand, and her gaze followed the sinews of his arm to his massive biceps and broad shoulder—muscles that no longer seemed like a sign of his vanity, but weapons in his arsenal. Despite all they'd been through, the shadows of his dimples remained and his wavy blond hair still looked boyishly carefree, but the planes of his jaw were rigidly set and the expression on his face was one she'd never seen on him before— hard and dangerous.

He raised his eyes and caught Camille staring. She wrenched her gaze to the window, her whole upper body flushing hot.

The guard moaned, snapping Camille back to the moment. She lunged for his gun at the same time Aaron did, but he reached it first. The guard moaned again before Aaron knocked his head with the butt of the rifle, sending him out cold once more.

Camille searched the men for weapons and discovered a short-barreled .38 Special. She spun the cylinder to check for bullets, which was no easy task given the way her hand shook. *Here we go,* she thought, snapping the fully loaded cylinder in place. The last thing she wanted to do was reveal this weakness to Aaron.

You see, I have this condition called post-traumatic stress disorder...

She cringed. Then she had an idea. "Aaron, you mind trading guns?"

He *tsk*ed in protest, but held the rifle out. "I guess size really does matter to a lady."

With the rifle, Camille felt better. She could hold it with both hands instead of one and steady it against her shoulder when she fired. Besides, one didn't need to strive for accuracy with an M16. She slung the gun's strap over her head and pushed the rifle around to her back. Squatting, she removed the guard's shoes and black jeans.

"What are you doing?" Aaron asked.

"I hate wearing skirts." She unzipped the offensive garment and pushed it down an inch before remembering her audience. Aaron's face was frozen in a grimace. So she disgusted him, what else was new? She couldn't escape shoeless, wearing a skirt. "Do you mind?"

"Do I mind that you're about to put on those nasty pants? Hell, yeah. They look like a biological superweapon."

"No, wise guy. Do you mind giving me some privacy?"

He faced the wall. Ignoring the foul odor wafting from the pants, Camille donned them and folded the waist to help with the fit.

"You can turn around now."

She tried on the other man's sneakers and was grateful they were a near fit.

"That's quite a look you've created."

She brought the rifle forward, gripping it tightly with both hands to keep the shaking to a minimum. "Yeah, I'm a real fashion maven. I'm calling this look *Cartel Chic*."

Aaron chuckled and Camille surprised herself by joining in. She did look pretty awful.

Too soon, the moment passed as they remembered where they were and what they'd done. Both sets of eyes returned to the unconscious figures on the ground.

"That was almost too easy," Camille said.

"We're not done yet, Blondie. We still have to escape from the compound."

Chapter 4

Camille was ready. She rolled her shoulders and felt the slide of her muscles against her camisole. Maybe it was only the effect of the adrenaline surging through her system, but she felt her position of power all the way to her toes. This random fate that had befallen her, to die at the hands of a bunch of criminals for a cause that wasn't her own, was about to get the shaft.

She walked to the door. "Ready?"

Aaron stood behind her, the .38 Special brushing her shoulder. "Let's do it."

She opened the door a crack, listening. A television set blared from the direction she and Aaron had been brought into the building, with a woman shouting in Spanish like a game show announcer might, against a background of hooting and cheers from an audience. Unable to hear anything above the din, she nosed her head through the doorway.

Somewhere nearby, a door banged closed. Camille flinched and pulled back, listening until she picked up the barely audible sound of a man's voice amid the television's noise. Then a second person spoke. A child. At the sound of Rosalia's pixie voice, Camille ached. She wanted to scoop the little girl up and run with her back to California, straight to the loving arms of her mother. But instead of acting impetuously and getting them all killed in a firefight, the best she could do for Rosalia was escape and tell U.S. authorities where to find her. Still, it was heart wrenching to leave her behind.

They crept into the hallway and turned right, toward three closed doors. It felt like Russian roulette, picking a door to open not knowing who or what was on the other side, but they had no other options.

Camille turned the knob of the first door. Aaron placed a hand on the small of her back and the barrel of his gun on her shoulder, angling it through the opening. She scanned the darkness. Someone slept on a cot along the wall. He stirred and rolled on his side. Holding her breath, she closed the door.

They tiptoed to the next room, though the blaring television program masked the sound of their movement. Aaron placed his hand on the doorknob. Camille wasn't tall enough to aim her weapon over his shoulder, so she slid it along his side, under his arm. The knob turned; the seconds ticked by. Aaron stuck his face through the crack. He smiled at Camille and stepped inside. Camille followed, closing the door behind her.

This room was not as dark as the first. The window was uncurtained and unbarred. A row of wooden crates identical to those pushed out of the plane sat along one wall, stacked two high.

On another wall stood a table weighed down with piles of American cash.

Camille walked to the crates and tried to lift one. "Help me with this."

"What are you doing?"

"These guys are weapons smugglers, right? So what do you think's in these boxes, donations to Goodwill?"

"You guard the door. I'll look inside." He tucked the gun into his waistband. Camille tried to ignore the zing of desire that hit her at that maneuver. What a stupid thing to think about when their lives were in danger. On second thought, it was a stupid thing to think about *at any time*. She had no business *ever* thinking about Aaron's pants or what he put in them.

He lifted a box to the ground and dumped packing peanuts on the floor.

"This was the best idea you've ever had, Blondie."

With her rifle aimed at the closed door, she walked backward until she stood over the box.

Aaron was right. This was the best idea she'd ever had. She didn't even care that he'd called her that terrible name again because in the box, nestled in a black nylon bag, were ten Smith & Wesson M&P 9 mm pistols. With silencers. And boxes of ammunition.

Aaron moved the .38 from the front of his waistband to the back. He screwed a silencer on to a 9 mm and loaded the magazine. Repeating the process with a second pistol, he handed it to Camille. She tucked it into her jeans.

"Don't you want to trade up for the silent model?" Aaron asked with honest surprise.

Camille wasn't about to admit her gun-handling defect. "Like you said, size matters."

He snorted and moved the bag to the table. "I'll look in the next box. You load this with cash."

They set to work. Within the span of a few minutes, their luck had improved tenfold. Instead of two guns with limited ammunition, they now had two AR-15 assault rifles, four 9 mm pistols with silencers, countless rounds of ammo, four grenades and—by Camille's hasty count—two hundred and fifty thousand U.S. dollars.

The grenades were an interesting find. Camille would have had no moral qualms against blowing up the compound and everyone in it if Rosalia hadn't been present. Then she had another idea. It would be extremely risky, but still, it might work.

"Aaron, are there any more grenades in those boxes?"

The woman had balls, figuratively of course. Aaron was sure he couldn't have come up with a better plan if given a week to think about it. He rummaged through the boxes until he found another grenade, which he handed to Camille. Replacing the lid, he moved the box under the window to use as a step.

"I'll be right back," she whispered.

Her destination was across the hall, to the room that had been their prison. They were about to kill two people and Aaron couldn't find it in his heart to be upset. He was more disturbed that it didn't bother him.

Rifle in hand and the game-changing bag of booty slung over his shoulder, he stood on the box. From the looks of it, the rear wall of the house ran parallel to the western wall of the compound, with about three feet between the two. Plenty of room to jump and run.

Camille returned, sprinting through the door and kicking it shut as the grenade detonated. The explosion was earth-rattling. Aaron's ears rang and the door nearly came off its hinges. He slammed the rifle butt into the glass. He couldn't hear it break over the din of the explosion but felt the pane give way. After sweeping the rifle across the window to clear it of glass, he moved out of Camille's way.

In a flash of golden mane and lithe limbs, she jumped out the window. Aaron landed behind her and they ran, staying low under the windows along the north side of the building. Aaron peered around the corner at the crowd in the courtyard surrounding the crater that used to be their hostage-holding room.

A five-foot gap loomed between the house and a shed. Though Camille's ruse was working, it was still a leap of faith to zip between the buildings in plain sight. If only one man looked in their direction, they were dead. Aaron went first, holding his breath for the three steps it took to make the pass. They followed the path of the compound wall to the end of the shed, which still left them with a solid two car lengths of empty space to reach the entrance gate.

A burly man with a full beard and a rifle was standing inside the locked gate, yelling and gesturing to the men at the explosion site. Aaron knew what needed to be done and said a prayer for forgiveness. He'd never been a particularly religious man, but he was about to murder someone point-blank. At least with the grenade, Aaron didn't have to watch anyone die. This time, though, he was going to look a man in the eyes and shoot him.

"I got this." He picked up a rock and threw it against the wall, waiting for the guard to investigate. His heart pounded out of control and his hands were sweaty, but he wiped them on his jeans and manned up. Their lives depended on this and he wasn't going to act like a sissy by getting all shaky and nervous.

The guard's shadow gave him away first. His stomach came into view, then his arms and gun. Aaron fired two rounds, one into his head and the other into his chest. Though the sound of the shots was blunted by a silencer, the *plunk plunk* still echoed between the shed and the compound wall.

Aaron worked hard to ignore the significance of what he'd done as he frisked the dead man for keys, finding them in a pants pocket.

"Anyone onto us?" he asked Camille, who had chanced a look around the corner.

"We're good. They're putting out a fire on the roof."

"Then we keep moving." He sprinted to the gate

with a key in his outstretched hand. *Please let this be the right key....*

It was not. He jerked the key out of the padlock. His fingers found the next key on the loop and jammed it into the lock. It gave way this time. The chain dropped to the ground and they were through.

Aaron's and Camille's feet slipped on the loose gravel, but they maintained their breakneck speed to the lean-to. While he ran, Aaron scanned the half dozen horses. The dark brown steed appeared to be the healthiest of the bunch, with muscular legs that looked ready to fly over the terrain. He skidded to a stop and dropped their cache to the ground.

Camille was right behind him. "Okay, you're the horse expert. Go for it."

He hunted through a crate for a saddle, blanket, bridle and harness, and made quick work of readying the horse to ride. The memory of Camille's struggle to mount their last horse was still fresh in his mind, so he grabbed her around the waist and tossed her up.

She yelped in protest.

Aaron pushed the bag of guns and money onto her lap, then swung up behind her. "If I'm in charge, then we're doing this my way."

Camille must have thought better about arguing because she silently lifted herself from the saddle so he could get comfortable, then settled onto his groin as she had the day before. Aaron reached around her, grabbed the reins and spurred the horse into a gallop.

Their destination was east, to the ocean. Once the compound was no longer visible, he slowed the horse, setting a reasonable pace to conserve the animal's energy in the stifling, midmorning heat.

Aaron loved to ride and had been doing so since he could walk. There weren't many activities for desert kids like him in a one stoplight town, but he had the State Park at his doorstep. His parents took full advantage of that fact and made sure he and his younger sisters could ride and hike like pros.

Miles of desert disappeared behind them. Their steed easily avoided the thick blanket of shrubs and giant cardón cacti, which stood with long, green arms reaching for the sky like an army a thousand strong. Aaron found no signs of human existence, just acres and acres of pristine wilderness.

Camille's hair was as untamable as the land. It whipped and tickled Aaron like a cruel taunt. Unable to resist, he covetously gathered it in his free hand. He was such a fool to do that. A certifiable idiot. But he did it anyway, burying his nose in the locks before letting them slip through his fingers to blow in the wind.

Camille hadn't noticed, and while he was relieved, her obliviousness made him greedier. He felt himself harden and hoped she was oblivious to that, too. He gathered her hair again and glimpsed the creamy skin of her neck. His mouth watered at the thought of kissing it, which was even more certifiably idiotic, given that Camille was heavily armed.

At that inopportune moment, their horse lurched and he accidentally tugged her hair.

"What are you doing?"

"Trying to get your hair out of my face," he replied gruffly.

"Oh, sorry." She twisted it and stuck it down her shirt. "That's the best I can do for now."

That solved the hair problem. Now how was she going to stop the friction of her hips rocking against him or the agonizing heat passing from her body to his?

She relaxed against him, wiggling her backside as she settled. Choking back a groan, he looked heavenward, hoping they'd reach the ocean soon. He needed to get off this horse before he did something he'd spend the rest of his life regretting.

Aaron would never forget his first time meeting Camille at Juliana and Jacob's engagement party, though not for its pleasantness. Aaron had taken one look at her standing on his parents' patio and targeted her as his next bedmate.

Like the fool he was around pretty girls, he cranked up his charm wattage, swaggering and openly praising her voluptuous attributes. And there was a lot to praise about Camille's body. She was, without a doubt, one of the most beautiful women he'd ever laid eyes on, with legs that went on for miles, curves custom-made for a man to wrap his hands around and full, pouty lips. Then she opened them and it was all downhill from there.

Apparently, his charm was too much for Camille to handle because the more charismatic he was, the more pungent she became. After that party, they'd seen enough of each other to last a lifetime. Aaron decided that no woman, no matter how stunning, was worth battling with such a sour disposition.

He smiled at the memory and might have laughed except Camille would want to know what was so funny. He'd thought about it in the plane and it struck him again how ironic life could be. He was racing across the Mexican desert with the only woman he'd wished to never see again.

And he was more attracted to her than ever.

Finally, the horse crested a ridge overlooking the beach. A temperate ocean breeze puffed at them, cooling Aaron's sunburned skin.

"We should ride in the surf to erase our tracks, in case they're on our trail," Aaron said as their mount picked its way down a canyon.

"Which direction do you think we should go?"

"If my bearings are correct, then the city we saw when we jumped is to the south. Let's see what we find." He tugged the reins.

Ahead of them stretched a pristine yellow-sand beach edged by cliffs and the endless ocean, which sparkled in the bright afternoon sun. It was lovely, really. Only a few hours earlier, he'd faced his own death, yet now he was riding horseback with a gorgeous woman along an empty beach. He closed his eyes and basked in the moment. Then the butt of Camille's rifle poked him in the ribs.

"You know, when I fantasize about riding with a woman through the surf in Mexico, she's not usually carrying a rifle."

She twisted to look at him, wearing a wicked grin on her lips. "Sounds like you have boring fantasies."

Aaron threw his head back and laughed. Leave it to Camille to surprise him again. He thought of a good comeback, something snarky and full of innuendo, but decided against voicing it. *This is good enough for now.*

He settled his arms more comfortably around Camille's sides, took another furtive inhale of her hair's magnificent scent and looked to the horizon, waiting for any vestiges of civilization to come into view.

Not five minutes later, he heard, then saw, an approaching vehicle in the distance. With a quiet curse, he turned their horse toward the cliffs lining the beach and found a concave section of cliff face. They dismounted, firearms ready. Besides the roar of the vehicle's engine, Aaron heard voices whooping and hooting. *Odd...*

He tipped his face around the corner. "It's a Jeep with at least four people."

"Why are they shouting?" Camille asked.

"I have no idea."

"I hear something else, too. What *is* that?"

Aaron shook his head. "I can't quite make it out."

They stood and listened. Aaron glanced at Camille's hands, which had started to shake, but decided against asking her about it.

The sound that had been so faint over the thunder of the waves and the hollering and the Jeep's engine became clearer to Aaron. "It sounds like… huh?"

He and Camille looked at each other, their faces screwed up in confusion.

"Bruce Springsteen?" they exclaimed in unison.

Chapter 5

"Hide the guns. No way are these people cartel hit men." Aaron held the bag open and Camille wedged her rifle inside. She flexed her fingers, the weight on her chest lighter with the gun out of her hands.

The Jeep hurtled toward them, spitting sand in its wake and blasting Bruce Springsteen. Aaron grabbed the bag and the horse's reins. Walking the horse behind them, they planted themselves in the path of the joyriders. The music went dead and the Jeep crawled to a stop a few yards in front of them.

The man behind the wheel looked about fifty,

with gray streaks in his brown hair, a softened body and the laid-back disposition of a man embracing his inner-Jimmy Buffett. The two women in the backseat looked young and were exactly the type of cupcakes Camille had railed against that morning. Clad in bikinis topped with cover-ups that didn't actually cover anything up, they were overdone in every way—too much makeup, too many artificial highlights in their hair and massive designer sunglasses.

"Hello there," the driver said. "You two look like you might need some help. Am I right?"

Aaron answered. "You guessed it. We came down to Baja with friends to go camping and when we left on our horse for a ride along the beach, they ditched us."

"They don't sound like very good friends."

"No kidding," Aaron said.

The driver rubbed his goatee. "Tell you what. We're pretty close to our camp. Would you and your girlfriend care to follow us back? I bet we could rustle up a cell phone for you to call your friends, and you can have a bite to eat and let your horse rest."

"I think we're done with those particular friends. Maybe we could borrow that phone to make other arrangements?"

"We can do that, too."

"Thank you." Aaron smiled wolfishly at the cupcakes. "Oh, and for the record, Camille and I are only friends. We're not…"

"Friends riding together on a horse?" one of the cupcakes asked.

"Yeah, her horse took off. We didn't have a choice."

Camille shifted her gaze to the rusty brown cliff face, regrouping. It wasn't that she cared about Aaron's enthusiastic clarification that they weren't involved—it was the truth, after all. And she didn't mind that the girls were angling for a better view of him. He was the most magnificent-looking man she'd ever seen, too. It was just that she was disappointed to have been wrong about him.

Since being taken hostage, she'd started to believe he'd changed, that underneath his party-boy persona was a respectable man capable of so much more than preening and seducing women. She'd begun to think of the two of them as a team. But she'd been wrong and the misjudgment stung. But she had more important issues to worry about than a man so easily distracted by pretty girls.

Her thoughts returned to Rosalia, alone and frightened in the compound. Camille hadn't considered it before, but maybe she'd been dropped in the middle of the Mexican desert for a reason. Maybe this journey wasn't another case of her rotten luck, but a chance to redeem thirty wasted years. Maybe she needed Rosalia as much as the little girl needed her. A new plan began to take shape in her mind.

The driver offered his hand to shake. "The name's Charlie. In the back we've got Ana and Sarah."

"I'm Aaron and this is Camille." He waved to the cupcakes, and added a wink for good measure.

Unbelievable.

Charlie must have noticed Camille's discomfort because he patted her hand. "Would you like to ride with us? We have room."

His palm was sweaty and his fingers bloated, but he might prove to be a valuable component to her plan.

"Thank you, Charlie." And though she wanted to yank her hand away and wipe it on her pants, she gave his fingers a little squeeze. She even pulled off a convincing smile.

He wasn't being manipulative—that was such an ugly word—but Aaron knew how to be persuasive to women. He knew what they wanted to hear, what little looks and touches would turn them to putty in his hands. Except for Camille. Nothing softened her, but that was beside the point.

As soon as Aaron saw the women in the Jeep, he knew they were his and Camille's ticket out of Mexico. All he needed was a little time with them to parse out the details. He regretted Camille's embarrassment when he distanced himself from her, but he needed the women to think he was available, not some letch trying to cheat on his girlfriend.

Charlie's eyes had turned hungry at the revelation he and Camille weren't an item. Aaron hadn't counted on that. She'd already proved she could kick ass and take names, but it went against his basic instincts to throw any woman to the wolves, even a cop.

Not that she seemed to mind. She was laughing and making flirty eyes at Charlie while Aaron was forced to watch through the rearview mirror as he followed the Jeep on horseback. Charlie wasn't remotely attractive and he was at least twenty years her senior. He seemed like a nice guy, sure, but as spineless as they came. A man like that could no more handle a woman like Camille than a child could handle a pet tiger.

The camp, though visible from the beach, was nestled into a valley between two foothills and demarcated by two palm-thatched palapas on the beach. One shaded a hammock. Aaron followed the Jeep onto a dirt road that wound among the homes, if he dared use such a polite word to describe the dwellings. Reeking of seaweed, the after-odor of bonfires and marijuana, the settlement was the housing equivalent of a pack of stray dogs. Of the twenty or so places, some were less flea-bitten than others, a few even looked rather domesticated, but the whole lot of them was a mangy bunch of misfits.

Charlie directed Aaron to the sea-green shack of some absentee neighbors who often brought their horse with them. Sure enough, a wood-and-wire fenced corral was sandwiched on the side of the property. No doubt the animal would be well cared for here. It didn't seem to have any identifying marks that might prove dangerous if the cartel went on the prowl for their stolen horse, which was a small blessing. To repay this community with the wrath of a vengeful cartel would be unforgivable.

The hardworking horse had one task left before

it could rest, though. Aaron tugged the reins and set off for the perimeter of the settlement to take note of all the paths leading to and from the camp, should they need to make a quick getaway. Jacob would've said it was Aaron's Golden Ticket at work again, but nevertheless, Aaron was relieved to discover only one access point from the west, a steep dirt road leading out of the valley. Perfect.

He returned to the corral, found feed and grooming supplies and set to work tending the horse.

"You're a sneaky man," a heavily accented female voice behind him said. Ana, if he remembered correctly. "We've been looking everywhere for you."

Seducing these women would be a piece of cake if they were going to throw themselves at him. He kept scrubbing, to see how hard they'd work to get his attention. "Responsibility before pleasure, as they say."

"How sensible of you," she purred. A darkly tanned Latina, she was taller than Sarah and looked to be in her late twenties, with long black hair and a temptress's body. Not too long ago, Aaron might have quit his job and moved to Mexico for the promise of this woman's company. But his responsibility to Camille and his desire to make it out of Mexico alive superseded everything else.

"This horse worked hard today. It deserves a little pampering."

"I think I'm jealous of the horse," Sarah, obviously American judging by her voice, said. A pair of trim, tan legs came into view, complete with a Tinker Bell ankle tattoo. Aaron let his gaze roam over her body, hoping she couldn't tell how artificial his perusal was.

"When you're done here, would you like to freshen up at our place? We have a cell phone you can use to make those other arrangements you mentioned," Ana said.

"That would be wonderful. Speaking of other arrangements, how far from the city are we?"

"We're fifty miles north of La Paz, where we're from."

The women watched him clean the horse's hooves. "Fifty miles isn't so bad. I'm thinking my friend and I could hitch a ride with someone and come back for the horse with a trailer."

"We'd be happy to give you and your friend a ride. We're going home tomorrow afternoon."

So far, so good. He put away the grooming supplies and gave the horse a second generous scoop of food.

"I'm ready to get cleaned up. Lead the way."

Sarah and Ana took him by the arms. As they strolled, Aaron asked, "Which one of you owns the house?"

Sarah answered. "Ana's brother owns it. He lets us use his place anytime we want."

"What kind of work do you do?"

"We're both high school teachers, English," Ana said.

"I'm from Arizona," Sarah explained. "I'm teaching here on an exchange program."

"It's a good thing I never had teachers like you two. I would have been a terrible student."

"Why is that?" Ana asked, giving his arm an extra squeeze.

"Just so you'd keep me after class."

The women giggled right on cue. At that moment, Camille came into view, standing by herself in front of Charlie's powder-blue trailer. She tracked his movement with wary eyes.

"Here's our place." Ana led him to a cottage across the courtyard from Charlie's house.

He glanced over his shoulder at Camille. A wrinkle of worry had appeared between her eyebrows. Reluctantly, he turned his back on her and climbed the rickety wooden porch steps. He sure hoped she was smart enough to figure out he hadn't abandoned her.

Loneliness wasn't a new emotion for Camille, but one that hit her hard as she watched the door close behind Aaron. Loneliness and betrayal. She stared at the door for a long time while she reined in her emotions and considered her next move.

A hand brushed her shoulder. Her reaction was

instinctive and immediate. Angling her elbow at a point, she whirled to jab her assailant in the stomach.

"Whoa." Charlie jumped back with his arms up in surrender.

"Sorry. I'm a little on edge today."

"No harm done. Where'd you learn a move like that?"

"Self-defense class. A girl can't be too careful these days."

"Right you are. I came to ask if you wanted to get cleaned up at my humble abode."

"Thanks. That would be wonderful."

He pointed to the black bag at Camille's feet. "I'm guessing you don't have a change of clothes in there."

"No. I wish."

"Well, last year a lady friend came to stay with me, but she left in a huff." He smiled as though recalling a private joke. "Didn't take her suitcase. I bet you could find something to fit you."

Camille nodded, grateful for the opportunity

to shed the nasty jeans. "Thank you, not only for the clothes, but for giving us a place to regroup."

"It's not often a man stumbles on a lovely young lady in need of rescuing." He draped an arm across her shoulders and guided her to his house.

Camille tried to fit the image Charlie had of her by acting sweet and demure. She wasn't used to playing the unsavory role of a damsel in distress but had a lot riding on his belief that she was. Maybe he'd forget she tried to gut him with her elbow.

At sunset, Aaron sat in a white plastic patio chair and wolfed down a second plate of food at the traditional Saturday night communal barbecue. Strands of white lights rimmed the sprawling courtyard and classic rock filtered out through the windows of Charlie's trailer. Twenty or so people were in attendance, mostly adults with a few kids thrown in. Charlie manned a charcoal grill on his porch with a beer in his hand.

The shower Aaron took at the teachers' cottage had been a godsend and Ana had allowed him to rummage through her brother's closet for clothes. Though he was still exhausted, at least he was clean and fed. He hadn't seen Camille since freshening up and was beginning to feel uneasy about her absence. He had no time to look for her, though, because the teachers didn't grant him the tiniest bit of breathing room. As though in competition, they seemed afraid to leave him alone lest the other one gain the advantage.

He frowned as he scanned the crowd for the thousandth time. Camille had another five minutes to materialize before he went in search of her.

"What do you think? Aaron, are you listening?" It was Ana.

"Ask me again?" He'd have to be more attentive if he expected Ana to offer Camille and him a ride to La Paz the next day. Borrowing Sarah's phone earlier, he'd briefly touched base with Dreyer to explain what happened and where they were. Then the teachers were back in the room, preening and posing, and he'd hung up after agreeing to wait in La Paz for further instruction on the safest and most discreet way for ICE to get them out of the country.

"I asked, what do you think of our little vacation spot?"

"I've never seen another place—"

At that moment, Camille appeared out of the darkness. She filled a plate from the buffet table and took a seat on the edge of the courtyard. Aaron's relief at seeing her hit him hard enough that he sighed audibly. She'd changed into a floral skirt and a red tank top, which were terrible clothing choices. Not only was the skirt impractical, but if she was trying to be inconspicuous, this was not the top she should've chosen. Couldn't she have found a baggy sweatshirt to borrow?

Ana traced his line of sight to Camille and stood. "Enough talk. It's time to dance."

She led him onto a clear section of concrete where a few other couples swayed to the music. Sarah followed close at their heels. Camille was grimacing at her food and had yet to acknowledge his existence, which bothered him, although he wasn't sure why. He wasn't acknowledging her either, which he decided to correct after the next song ended.

Ana and Sarah danced against him with borderline desperation. Sarah wasted no time making sure Aaron knew precisely what she wanted from him. When grinding against him failed to hold his attention, she threw her arms around his neck and caught him in a surprise kiss.

Her breath reeked of cigarettes and tequila, like the girls in the dance clubs all smelled. Disgusting. But Sarah was the one with the cell phone and he needed to make a second expensive international call to Jacob later that night, so he kissed her back. When Sarah let go of him and Ana took her place, his eyes found Camille again. She was still scowling at her untouched food.

He couldn't decide if she was nervous about the possibility of the cartel finding them or merely irritated that other people were enjoying themselves. Actually, it reminded him of the way she looked at Juliana and Jacob's wedding reception, as if she'd decided beforehand to have a bad time and resented the other attendees for choosing otherwise.

More than any other aspect of her personality, her tendency to act put-upon really pissed him off. If she could change that one thing about herself, she'd be the total package—beautiful, intelligent and fun to be around. But two out of three was like being served a decadent dessert covered in mold.

Sarah, cutting off his line of sight, ran her fingers through his hair and turned his face toward hers.

He forced a smile. "Think I'm going to take a break, ladies."

Ana slipped her foot up his leg. "Don't be too long. Sarah's been greedy for your attention and I'm starting to feel lonely."

Oh, brother. "I'm going to get a drink and borrow Charlie's facilities. When I get back, you and I will dance again."

At the drink table, he mixed a margarita in a plastic cup for Camille. He planned to stay stone-cold sober to keep a lookout for the cartel, but a little alcohol would be harmless for Camille and might help her sleep. At the very least, she might stop looking like someone ran over her dog.

He reached her chair and found it empty. Scanning the crowd, he spotted her on the dance floor, her arms around Charlie.

Charlie was a terrible dancer and his hands were way too close to Camille's butt to be gentlemanly. Aaron glared at them, trying to catch Camille's attention. What the hell was she thinking, throwing herself at a sweaty, middle-aged pothead while their lives were in danger?

At least her hair was in a ponytail. Crazy that it mattered to him, but if Charlie laid a finger on Camille's hair, Aaron wouldn't be able to stop himself from dragging her away and shaking some sense into her. As long as he and Camille were in Mexico, her hair belonged to him alone.

He huffed, disgusted as much by his train of

thought as the sight of Charlie's hands all over Camille. After downing the margarita, he crushed the cup and marched back to Ana, thumping Charlie's shoulder hard with his own as he passed.

Ana welcomed him with open arms. "You've come back to me."

"I have."

If anyone could distract him, it would be Ana, whose sexuality oozed like honey from a comb. He put his hands on her hips and pulled her hard against his thigh, moving them as a unit to the beat of the music. *To stop thinking about her for just one song, I'll push this as far as it will go.*

Camille hated dancing, always had. So it was hard to contain her revulsion when Charlie asked her to dance. But she couldn't say no, not when he'd agreed to loan her his Jeep the next morning.

At first, she was relieved that he initiated only the slightest sway of movement. Then she felt his hands getting friendly with her backside. As she smiled and made flirtatious conversation, she made a mental list of all the reasons why she was allowing herself to be treated in such a demeaning way. Still, the urge to break Charlie's hands made it challenging to maintain a facade of sweetness.

Halfway through the song, she looked over Charlie's shoulder and spotted Aaron walking in her direction. He sent her a murderous glare before wrapping one of the cupcakes around his body and practically screwing her right there on the dance floor. Like watching a car wreck in progress, Camille was powerless to look away.

Charlie, with a finger on her chin, forced her focus back to him. "He said you two weren't an item."

"Trust me, we're not."

"Then why are you jealous?"

"Oh, no. I'm not jealous. Just disappointed."

"Sometimes people don't turn out to be who we expect them to."

She wound her arms around Charlie's neck. "And some people are *exactly* who they first appear to be."

Charlie smiled. "You sure you don't want my help tomorrow looking for your lost horse?"

"Thank you, but I'd like to go alone. I'll bring some rope and tether it to the rear of the Jeep for the trip back to camp. I can't tell you how grateful I am for your help. I'm so lucky you found me on the beach." Stifling a cringe, she stroked his jaw and tried to fill her eyes with the promise of reward for his generosity.

A loud giggle from Aaron's groupies reclaimed Camille's attention. The American girl was attached to him again. Aaron must have said something really funny because both girls were tittering and playing with their hair.

That was enough for Camille. She kissed Charlie on the cheek. "It's my bedtime. Thanks for the dance...and the Jeep."

"You're welcome to sleep at my house, you know."

Nice try, buddy. "The beach beckons."

As soon as Charlie moved into conversation with another couple, Camille strode into Aaron's circle of hedonism and grabbed his arm. "Sorry to interrupt. I need to talk to Aaron. Don't worry, I'll return him to you in a sec."

She marched him by the elbow toward the water, where the sound of the waves would drown out their words, and spun to face him. "I've seen enough of your disgusting display."

"Aw, how sweet, you saved all your nastiness for me. Don't I feel special."

"If you want my advice, I think your best chance is with the American. She seems to have the lowest self-esteem of the two."

Aaron threw his arms skyward. "That's how little you think of me? You really believe that after all we've been through, I'm trying to get laid?"

"Isn't that what you're all about?"

"It shouldn't surprise me you feel that way."

She folded her arms across her chest. "What's that supposed to mean?"

"It means that your self-absorption distorts your perception of everyone else around you."

"You think *I'm* self-absorbed? No human being on the planet is more vain than you are."

"Are you kidding me? You've invested years in this whole martyr charade. Do you wake up feeling miserable or is that something you have to work up to over breakfast?"

It had been a long day. The ground looked fuzzy to Camille's weary eyes. Despite how well they worked together to escape the cartel's compound, interacting with Aaron was proving to be as toxic as ever. With what she was planning to do the next day, wasting her energy arguing with him was the last thing she needed.

She pinched the bridge of her nose. "You think your new friends will be willing to give you a lift to La Paz?"

He eyed her suspiciously. "They've already offered, and I accepted on both our behalf."

"Good. ICE will get you home safely from there." It was a burden off her mind that she didn't have to worry about him making it to California in one piece. Knowing Aaron had ICE backing him up, she could better concentrate on her plan.

"What's going on, Camille? Why are you talking like you're not coming with me?"

She straightened, trying to look as strong as she wished she felt. "Because I'm not. This is where we part ways. I'll only take my fair share of the money and weapons. The bag's behind the couch on Charlie's porch." What more could she say? It was great being kidnapped with you? "I've got a lot to do tomorrow, so I'm going to get some rest. Take care of yourself."

She took a step back. The cool sand trickled into the sandals Charlie loaned her.

"Camille, what the hell are you talking about?"

"Goodbye, Aaron."

She slunk sideways around his broad body, being careful not to touch him or smell his clean-laundry scent. Without looking back, she walked into the darkness.

Chapter 6

Feeling Aaron's eyes on her, Camille trudged through the sand to a hammock she spied earlier beneath a palapa. Was he relieved to be rid of her? Maybe, but what a dismal thought. She couldn't afford to dwell on the cruelty of the world, on what she'd lost and what she could never have.

She didn't need Aaron, she reminded herself. She didn't need anyone.

The hammock rocked as Camille sat, removed the band from her hair and ran her fingers through the hopelessly tangled tresses. If she survived until she reached La Paz, she'd cut it all off—a present to herself for beating the odds, which were perilously stacked against her.

She moved the pistol to her stomach for easy access during the night. With a yawn, she settled back with an arm behind her head.

A figure loomed over her. Camille gasped and grabbed for the gun, but Aaron disarmed her handily.

He crossed his arms and frowned at her. "What, specifically, do you have planned for tomorrow?"

With the express purpose of making him go away, she decided to give it to him straight. "I was leading Charlie on so he'd loan me his Jeep."

"Why?"

"I've decided to return to the compound to gather intel. The more data I can pass to U.S. authorities, the better Rosalia's odds for rescue. Then I'll drive the Jeep to La Paz and contact my team in the States to report my findings and get our families into protective custody so the cartel can't hurt them to punish us. What happens after that depends on what my bosses want me to do toward her rescue. But I've decided I'm not leaving Mexico until Rosalia's safe and I've done everything possible to help bring down the Cortez Cartel."

His scowl deepened. "I've already contacted my ICE team about Rosalia and protection for our families."

"You made a phone call? How?"

"Sarah let me borrow her cell phone. ICE has agents that specialize in rescue ops—to get both Rosalia and us out of Mexico. Look, it's virtually impossible to bring down a cartel. If it could be done, then the U.S. government would have already, trust me. There's no need to put yourself in more danger."

Camille gave a hard laugh. "*More danger?* You're kidding, right? We couldn't possibly put ourselves in any more danger if we tried. Even after Rosalia's rescued, do you honestly think the cartel will leave us alone? Do you think they stood around the hole from the grenade explosion and said to each other, 'They stole our money and guns and escaped. Oh, darn.'" She shook her head. "Aaron, they know who we are and where to find us. Maybe living in WitSec with your family for the rest of your life is acceptable to you, but it's not to me. I'm going to stay and fight."

Aaron was quiet for a long time. He dropped his arms and looked at the ocean.

To fill the silence, Camille kept talking. "I don't care if you think I'm doing it because I'm bent on being a martyr or whatever your opinion is of me. Rosalia deserves better. And I do, too. I may have a crappy life, but it's mine and I won't have a bunch of criminals dictating the terms. Maybe I'll end up a legend on the force like my old man after all."

He rubbed his chin, nodding. "What time do we leave in the morning?"

"What?"

"I'm in. What time do we leave?"

"What do you mean you're in? You're not invited."

"Have you ever driven off-road?"

"No, but—"

"I happen to be an expert at that. What time do we leave?"

Camille sighed. Of course the Golden Boy was an expert at off-roading. "Before dawn."

Aaron returned her gun and walked away, toward the party and his nubile teachers.

"I don't need you, Aaron," she called after him.

He turned around and walked backward through the sand, wearing a hard smile. "Yeah, well, I don't need you either, but here we are."

The breezeless beach was heavy with moist, salty air as Aaron maneuvered the Jeep over the sand in the predawn darkness. "I'm going to retrace our escape route to make sure I can find the compound again."

Yawning, Camille nodded her consent and ran a hand over the blue T-shirt and yoga pants she'd pilfered from Charlie's stash of clothes the night before. Though still groggy, she had woken with no trouble, which was out of character for her. She was typically such a heavy sleeper that waking enough to drag herself out of bed was the most difficult part of her day.

Under the pretense of looking at the ocean, she studied Aaron. She liked him like this, not the arrogant rake he'd been last night, but a serious, focused man. She had the sinking suspicion she could spend many content hours studying the small wrinkles that textured his face and made him appear less debonair, more distinguished.

The sun punctured the hazy sky as Aaron turned west through a dry riverbed between the cliffs separating the beach from the desert. They drove away from the light and into the gray-black darkness of endless foothills, toward danger that left no guarantee of their survival.

"I called Jacob last night."

Camille grinned. "Are Juliana and the baby okay? Is it a boy or girl?"

"A girl. Alana Rose. Jacob and Juliana are tired and worried about us, but everyone's healthy and safe. With your dad's police connections, Juliana's hospital room went under immediate guard. They'll move to the secure location my family's at once they're cleared by the doctors. Everyone's pretty pissed about our choice to stay in Mexico, but Jacob agreed to overnight my passport and the purse you dropped in the hospital parking lot to La Paz. The package should reach the city by tomorrow morning."

"That could be really useful. Thank you."

"One more thing. I don't think we should steal the Jeep. Charlie could contact Mexican authorities, and the last thing we need is to be arrested for grand theft auto. Ana offered to give us a lift this afternoon. She even suggested we spend the night at her place. I think we should take her up on it."

Camille snorted. "Judging by the way you two were dancing last night, I feel safe assuming she wasn't including me in her sleepover invitation."

Ugh. Why did she go there? She had about as much impulse control as a teenager.

Aaron rolled his tongue over his teeth. "I'm sure

she has a sofa you can sleep on while she has her way with me in the bedroom. We'll try to keep the noise down."

Camille felt her face heat up and fixed her gaze on the foothills to her right.

"So…this is your first time in a foreign country?"

"Huh?" He made it sound as if they were on vacation.

"When I called Jacob, your sister said she didn't think you had a passport. Is this your first time out of the U.S.?"

"Yeah. I've always wanted to travel, but I've never had the time."

Aaron scoffed. "Never had time? That's a bunch of bull. People who really want to travel make the time."

"What a pretentious thing to say. I suppose you're a world traveler?"

"I've been around. Still plenty of places I want to see, though. What else is on your bucket list besides travel? Any goals or dreams?"

"You mean, besides surviving today?" She shrugged. "The only dream I ever had was to be a cop. As far as goals, I'm a member of the hundred-mile club at my gym. You know, people who swim the equivalent of a hundred miles of laps annually."

Aaron shook his head, frowning as if she'd given the wrong answer.

"Do my life choices offend you?"

"How old are you?"

"Just shy of thirty. How old are you?"

"Thirty-four. What about a boyfriend?"

"My love life is none of your business." Not that she'd ever had a love life to worry about.

"That's a no. Hmph." His frown deepened.

"What about you? Anyone special waiting for you at home?"

"No—and that's the way I like it. Monogamy's not my gig."

She chortled. "You're going to end up being one of those pathetic middle-aged men with a showy sports car and a twenty-year-old girlfriend. You know that, right?"

"Sounds fantastic." He ignored her conspicuous eye roll. "What about kids? Do you want to start a family of your own?"

"Why are you asking me all this stuff?"

"Answer the question, Camille."

"I don't know…maybe. But what's the point in hoping for something that may never happen? I'm done talking about this stuff. I don't appreciate what you're doing."

"What am I doing?"

"You're compiling a list of how pathetic my life is."

"I'm curious, that's all," he said.

"No more questions."

"Fine with me. We're getting close. Get your gun ready in case we run into any unfriendly search parties looking for us."

Camille armed herself and scanned their surroundings. The landscape looked like all the other foothills they'd traversed in the past few hours, rolling slopes carpeted with tall cacti and short, scrubby-looking trees. Before this week, she thought she had a good sense of direction. Out here, surrounded by nothing but monotonous desert, she wouldn't have stood a chance without Aaron's help, not that she was going to mention it. She was still smarting from his cringe-inducing questions.

Aaron parked the car and lifted the weapon bag to the ground, where they finished prepping their guns. Each would approach the compound with a rifle and two pistols, carrying a grenade in one pocket and extra ammo in the other. Their goal was to sneak near enough to get descriptions and numbers on the cartel operatives.

Camille closed her eyes and took a moment to remind herself why she was doing this—for herself, for her family, for Rosalia.

Lips brushed hers, accompanied by the scratch of stubble. Her eyes flew open. Aaron's brown eyes stared back, challenging her to resist his charm.

Or, possibly, to succumb to it.

Panicking, she tried to move away but Aaron maintained a firm hand against the small of her back. Evidently, all those muscles weren't just for show.

She socked him on the shoulder but he was unfazed, pushing his lips to hers while he stroked her jaw, coaxing it to relax and open. She refused, but found herself wondering about his tongue. All she had to do was part her lips and she bet he'd show her exactly how masterful his tongue was. She shivered, thinking about that tongue, those lips, his stubble abrading the skin above her lip, every hard, solid part of him. To her mortification, her nipples hardened in response.

What a nightmare.

It was all that talk about bucket lists that made him do it. That coupled with the fact that in the past forty-eight hours Aaron had stared down his own mortality more than once. He'd obsessed for two straight years about kissing Camille Fisher and here she was before him, her eyes closed, her face turned skyward, her luscious lips calling to him. Any minute, they could die. So why not go for it while he had the chance?

Now or never, man. If you want that kiss, you're just going to have to take it.

So he did.

And, good God, she felt better than he'd imagined, pressed to his body, even with her stubborn mouth refusing to yield. She raised her hand to his face, as if maybe she was trying to pry him away, but he knew she needed this moment of connection as much as he did. Taking her wrist in hand, he brought it behind her, tipping her back and thrusting her breasts against his chest.

Holy hell.

Then her mouth opened and he seized the opportunity to slip a finger between her parted lips, applying gentle pressure until—finally, *finally*—her mouth surrendered to his demand. Adrenaline coursed through him, leaving him breathless as he plundered the depths of her, demanding and exploring her warm, wet mouth. Memorizing the taste of her.

She slung an arm around his neck with a moan and something inside Aaron broke free. Crushing her supple, gorgeous body to his, he bowed her back even farther until they both teetered on the edge of falling.

When Aaron released Camille, he took a couple of swift steps back, probably fearful that she was going to knee him in the groin. Which she would have done had her legs not been so weak. She concentrated on staying upright and breathing. Keeping her eyes on Aaron, who seemed to be struggling toward that same end, a single, fleeting thought darted across her mind—she'd been right about his tongue.

As soon as she regained her composure, she shot him her best withering glare. "What the hell was *that?*"

"We might die at any time and I decided it would be nice to kiss you first."

She grabbed her rifle from the weapon bag. "Don't ever do that again."

"Yes, ma'am."

She didn't buy his easy concession for a second. The man looked about as remorseful as the Devil. He brushed past her, toward the peak of the hill. Still not sure her legs would carry her, she touched a finger to her swollen lips and watched Aaron walk. Then she realized she was staring at his perfect, firm backside. As if he were God's gift to women.

As if.

With a snort of disgust, she jogged to catch up.

"That's odd," Aaron whispered from where he lay on the ground at the top of the hill, his eyes on the valley to the west.

"What's odd?"

"No guard and no horses in the lean-to. In fact, I don't see a single person."

"Huh. Let me take a look." She left a good five feet of space between them as she army-crawled into a surveillance position. "There aren't any vehicles in the courtyard either." The place looked like a ghost town. Camille's hope disintegrated. Unbelievable. Could her luck get any worse? She kicked a rock and watched it tumble past the Jeep, down the hill.

"Let's go in for a closer look," Aaron said, his tone laced with disappointment. He blazed the way through a narrow canyon in tense silence.

They needn't have been quiet, though. Camille felt the vacancy in her bones as she neared the outer wall. She confirmed it after Aaron boosted her to look over the wall at the empty courtyard. No satellite equipment, no vehicles, nothing.

The hole created by the grenade explosion dominated the scene and offered a strange, grotesque view into the house where none should exist, like an eye socket without an eye. Burned bits of bone dotted the courtyard. Whether they were scattered by scavenging animals or the initial blast was a forensic question beyond Camille's knowledge set.

With their rifles ready, Aaron preceded Camille through the front gate. They opened the shed doors, then wandered into the house. The furniture had been left behind—sooty sofas in the living room, a scarred wooden table in the kitchen, unmade cots in the bedrooms. All the boxes had been cleared out of the weapon storage room.

Resolve—tenacious and angry—pierced through her disappointment, steeling her heart. Somewhere in this desert, a scared little girl needed saving. Camille wasn't about to let anything, even this seemingly insurmountable complication, derail her mission.

Returning to the courtyard, she found Aaron staring at the ground behind the shed, at the burned remains of the guard he'd shot and another poor soul who'd been added to the pyre.

"This doesn't change anything for me," she said, determination hardening her tone. "It makes it tougher, for sure, but I won't give up on Rosalia."

Aaron didn't say anything, didn't even nod. He just stared at the corpses.

Camille strode from the compound. Though her bum leg ached, she pushed the quarter mile to the

Jeep, hauling her body painfully over the steepest part of the hill as her adrenaline finally crashed. Damn, but her stupid leg was killing her. What she wouldn't give to prop it up on a sofa, down some ibuprofen and sleep for a day.

When she reached the Jeep, she braced her hands against the dusty metal frame. Too many thoughts crowded her brain for her to sit patiently while she waited for Aaron. Shifting her weight to her good leg, she picked up her left foot and kicked the rear tire with a bouncy rhythm. The sizzles of pain felt good. Necessary.

Charlie's clothes stash hadn't included any sneakers and so she wore the dead man's shoes today. She stared at them with disgust. Maybe she'd burn them tonight. Or throw them out the car window on the way to La Paz. Her first order of business in the city would be to buy herself an outfit or two. And she was definitely going to cut her hair.

She kept her eyes on her bouncing foot, affording Aaron's boots only a nominal glance when they appeared at her side. When the minutes stretched on and Aaron still didn't speak, she looked at him. Leaning against the Jeep, he watched her with a look that could only be described as sympathetic. As if she was a shelter dog or a beggar. It was illogical for him to feel that way because he was in the same boat as she was.

"Don't look at me like that."

"Like what?"

"Like you pity me."

"I do pity you."

"You're such a jerk." She pushed off the Jeep and put some space between them.

"Let me explain."

She whirled on him. "Do I have a choice?"

"That's my point."

"What are you talking about?"

"You haven't had a choice in any of this." His voice was firm, angry. "You were right last night, you know. Our number was up the second they took us hostage. We can never go home unless the cartel is miraculously destroyed. And here's the part that really gets me—they weren't even after you, Camille. You were literally in the wrong place at the wrong time. Like when you were shot. Wrong place, wrong time."

"You don't know anything about me or the accident."

"Jacob told me everything about the accident that ruined your career. About the shoot-out at the meth house you were raiding, how you two positioned yourselves in a bathroom but forgot to check the tub. I know about the little boy hiding inside, how he pulled Jacob's arm when he tried to fire into the hallway.

"He hit you instead. It about killed Jacob to watch you bleed out on the floor of that filthy bathroom while they secured the house. He said you didn't complain once. He said you insisted the paramedics take the boy away first."

"Any cop would've done the same."

"All you ever wanted to be in life was a police officer—you said it yourself today. That was your only dream and it died the day Jacob shot you.

Don't play me the fool by pretending your career is still on track. I know better."

"My past has nothing to do with this." She spread her arms, indicating the compound and the surrounding desert.

"You think one has nothing to do with the other? You don't think I notice your hand shake when you hold a gun? Or that your limp gets worse with every step you take? Your leg hurts pretty badly right now, doesn't it? Tell me I'm wrong."

"Shut up about how broken and pathetic I am."

"You're missing my point."

"Is that so? Because all I'm hearing is that you're a dirtbag."

"Camille, I pity you because you haven't experienced enough happiness. Your whole life has been one letdown after another. All responsibility and pain, no joy. And what do you do for fun? Swim back and forth in a pool?" He swiped a hand across his forehead. "You need a life, and I stole any chance you had for one. Any chance you had to find some happiness, *live a little,* was destroyed because the day Juliana went into labor, you got to the hospital at the same time I did. Wrong place, wrong time. Boom, your life is over. It's not fair."

Camille's insides had turned to fire. The exacting pain she usually felt with the memory of her accident was more akin to a match, igniting flames of rage that licked at her heart and lungs. She yelled with all the strength left in her. "Stop. Shut up. Just shut up."

She couldn't even see Aaron clearly, her eyes were so clouded by anger. She clenched her fists at her sides, trying to keep from attacking him like she wanted to.

Aaron took a tentative step toward her. "I pity you because you deserve so much more than the hand you've been dealt."

The pain in Camille's leg returned to her attention in full force. She was exhausted and hurt— physically and mentally. She sat where she stood, stretched out her left leg, drew her right knee in and rested her head in her arms. She didn't want to look at Aaron anymore. Or the vacant cartel compound. She didn't want to see the never ending desert or the brilliant blue sky.

"Camille, listen to me. You're the bravest person I've ever met. And I know a lot of men who've been in battle, a lot of men who go up against murderers every day. You trump them all. You don't let anything stand in your way, not a shaky trigger finger or a bum leg. I just… I respect that. You were caught up innocently in this whole mess, but without you, I'd probably be dead."

Camille's eyes brimmed with moisture to the extent that she stopped blinking, lest a drop jar loose to slip down her cheek.

"After everything you've been through in your life, you don't deserve to be in the middle of the Mexican desert fighting for the right to live peacefully. You should be in California holding your niece and getting your goddamned passport so you can start traveling." His voice was low but harsh. "You need to quit the effing police force and meet someone to start a family with—and spend every day for the rest of your life figuring out what makes you happy. Anything but this."

He exhaled deeply and paced in front of her.

Camille understood his argument. He pitied her mess of a life. How humiliating, but how true. There were so many times she could have curled in a ball and had her own pity party. But it wouldn't have done one bit of good—not then and not now either. She and Aaron needed to look to the future, to figure out how to rescue Rosalia and destroy the men who had marked them to die. They needed to deliver an epic cartel beatdown, not dissolve like a couple of wimps.

A rogue tear escaped from her eye.

"Don't you dare start crying," he commanded, stopping in his tracks and pointing a finger at her. "Or so help me, I'm going to hug you."

Camille smiled at the earnestness of his demand.

Aaron didn't return her smile, but offered her a hand. She accepted his help and didn't protest when he draped his arms over her shoulders.

"I'd insist that you let ICE take you home, and allow me to make things right for both of us, but I'm guessing you wouldn't go for that," he said.

"No way. We're in this together."

They stood, embracing, until the cry of a bird in the distance interrupted the moment. With nothing left to say, Camille walked around to the passenger side of the Jeep. She tried hard not to limp, but failed miserably.

Aaron, still looking at her way too seriously, opened her door. She let him, but as soon as he started the engine, she put her hand on the steering wheel to make sure she got his undivided attention.

"Aaron?"

"Hmm?"

"Don't ever pity me again."

"Yes, ma'am."

Then he smiled.

Chapter 7

With Baja's combination of dirt roads and pot-hole-riddled byways, it took Ana, in her ancient Pontiac hatchback, three hours to drive fifty miles. Three hours Camille spent in the backseat next to Sarah, who Camille hoped earned a backache the next day from constantly leaning forward to fondle Aaron's shoulders, neck and hair.

The city of La Paz unfolded gradually, with the occasional shack giving way to dirt roads lined with them. Ana's car thumped onto the first paved road after two hours of travel. The road gradually morphed into a bona fide highway and the real city started, with gray cinder-block houses and markets, auto repair garages and clothing stores sporting barred windows and half-empty shelves.

Throughout the drive, Aaron peppered Ana with questions about the city. La Paz had a population of roughly two hundred thousand people and sat on the southeast edge of the Baja peninsula at the back of a long, narrow bay fed by the Sea of Cortez, nine hundred miles south of the Mexican-American border and an ocean away from the Mexican mainland.

While the outlying sections of the city were relatively flat, the closer Ana drove toward the bay, the greater the downhill grade became, as if the whole of La Paz would eventually slip into the water. After going out of her way to give Aaron and Camille a mini-tour of the city, she turned away from the nicely maintained downtown district and into a less-picturesque urban neighborhood.

The houses were small and run-down, the streets narrow and jammed with parked cars. Save for the new Walmart and Costco Ana pointed out, this section of the city boasted no trendy shops like downtown, just taco stands and mini-marts, crumbling schools behind chain-link fences and drab apartment buildings. They dropped Sarah off in front of a freshly painted cottage with a weed-riddled yard and continued a few blocks more to Ana's apartment.

Camille hated the lack of security that came with arriving in broad daylight. After exiting the car, she scanned the sidewalks and apartment windows for sinister-looking faces. Nothing appeared out of the ordinary.

Ana chuckled at something Aaron said and for one sinking moment, Camille second-guessed their new friend's trustworthiness. What if Ana had ties to the Cortez Cartel? What if she and Aaron were walking into a trap?

Whoa there, girl. Deep breath.

So what if they might be ambushed by a bunch of Mexican mobsters? The faster she found the cartel, the sooner she'd rescue Rosalia. Besides that, it wasn't an ambush if she was armed and ready to fight back. With a hand on the grip of the gun in her pocket, she followed Aaron up a set of stairs to Ana's second-floor apartment.

Ana's place was small and tastefully decorated, with a living room that fit a sofa but little more and a bathroom that was only reachable through the single bedroom. Camille had the honor of using the bathroom first and let her eyes roam over the framed photos, knickknacks and books that topped Ana's dresser. She managed to resist the urge to rummage through the bathroom cabinets, a decision she felt quite mature about.

She returned to the kitchen several minutes later. "Okay, Ana, the bathroom's all yours."

"Thank you, Camille, but Aaron was about to explain why the front page of yesterday's newspaper contains a picture of you two being held at gunpoint."

Camille sank into a chair and angled for a view of the newspaper. The grainy color photo showed the two of them at their worst—snarling, caged animals that had been put through the wringer.

"You know." Aaron swatted the air with his hand. "Yesterday's news."

"The article claims you two are being held hostage by the Cortez Cartel. It seems that the cartel emailed your picture to both Mexican and American news sources and the American police, demanding that two men arrested earlier this week in California be released or they will kill you. Is it true? Were you kidnapped?"

"You'll be safer not knowing the details," Camille said.

"I deserve to understand the danger I bring into my home."

Aaron rose, wiping his palms on his jeans. "You're right about the danger. We'll show ourselves out."

Ana held her arm out to stop him. "Oh, no, you don't. I want answers or I'll call the police."

Camille had no idea why Ana didn't simply let them disappear into the night, but they couldn't afford any involvement from the Mexican police.

Aaron must have reached the same conclusion, because he dropped back into his chair.

"Start at the beginning," Ana said. "Why did the cartel kidnap you?"

Aaron did most of the talking and Camille was happy to let him. He wisely left out several details, including Rosalia's kidnapping, along with the fact that they'd already killed three cartel members and were planning to take down the rest. He also failed to disclose that they were armed to the teeth.

Ana nodded frequently and asked a couple of questions, but was otherwise nonplussed. "So, you're both American law enforcement?"

"Yes," Aaron said.

"Have you contacted your work or your families yet?"

"Yes, on both accounts."

"I'm sure your families are anxious for your return. Perhaps you need a ride to the airport tonight?"

"Actually," Aaron hedged, "we're planning to

stay in La Paz and gather intelligence on the cartel."

Ana covered Camille's hands with her own. "Remaining here would be very unsafe for you. The cartel—it is everywhere and it is merciless. If it finds you, you will die."

A tingle of fear crept over Camille's limbs, but she squelched it immediately. Her fear was nothing compared to what Rosalia must be experiencing. Besides, she and Aaron had already gone up against the cartel and survived. They could—and would—do so again, as many times as it took to secure Rosalia's freedom as well as their own.

"It's a risk we're prepared to take," she answered Ana. Aaron nodded his solidarity.

"Then I will help you as much as I can. You may stay with me as long as you need to."

"Thank you for the generous offer," Camille answered, "but one night is enough. Tomorrow the plan is for Aaron to find us a place to stay while I pick up supplies, then we'll be out of your way."

"Then tomorrow you may borrow my car to run errands. Sarah can drive me to work."

"But why would you put your safety at risk for us?" Camille added, sincerely baffled.

"You want to fight against the smugglers who bring guns into my country. It is an issue close to my heart. Let's leave it at that."

It was liberation time. While Aaron showered, Ana found a pair of scissors and a box of hair dye left over from the time she'd streaked her hair with red highlights. The chocolate-colored dye was a safety net in case she'd hated the highlights, which she hadn't.

"I've always wanted short hair," Ana whispered with conspiratorial enthusiasm. "Good for you."

Camille sat on a kitchen chair with a towel around her neck. "That page one color photo of me is reason enough for a change."

Ana picked up the scissors and made dramatic snipping motions in the air. Hopefully she'd be more prudent with the cut than her demonstration threatened. "Ready?"

"I've been ready for years." *Good riddance.*

"Stop! Oh my God. Are you crazy?" Aaron stomped from the bedroom with wet hair, clad in the same clothes he'd worn that day. He strode to Ana, snatched the scissors from her and chastised both women with furious eyes.

"Aaron, calm down. The cartel will be looking for a woman with long blond hair. It'd be stupid for me to leave it like that. And honestly, I can't wait to be rid of it. The only reason I kept it long was so I could put it in a bun for work. I think I'll look good as a short-haired brunette."

"Brunette?" He spit the word out as if it was a piece of gristle.

Camille pointed to the box of hair dye on the table.

Aaron's face twisted into a look of pure horror. He grabbed the box of dye, stuffed the scissors in his pocket and stomped to the front door. "Wear a hat."

He left, slamming the door behind him.

Camille shot a questioning look at Ana. "What was that about?"

"I think he likes your hair the way it is." Was that a hint of a smirk on Ana's face?

"What I do with my hair is none of his business. Do you have another pair of scissors we can use?"

Ana shook her head. "He took my only pair. You two are entertaining, you know that?" Oh, yeah, Ana was definitely smirking.

"I have no idea what you mean."

"I know, and that's why it's so amusing." Ana pulled the towel from around Camille's neck. "I have the perfect hat for you to borrow. Let's go look."

Adding scissors and hair dye to her mental grocery list for the next day, she allowed Ana to pull her by the arm to the bedroom closet.

The streets of La Paz bustled with activity now that the heat of the day had given way to a temperate evening. Aaron pulled his newly purchased ball cap low over his eyes and emerged from a corner market, his other purchases in hand. He ducked onto a quiet side street packed with towering, narrow houses and sat curbside in the shadow of a parked car.

He ripped the plastic covering from one of the two prepaid cell phones as he organized his thoughts. If he played this next conversation perfectly, he'd have ICE's considerable resources at his disposal for the duration of his and Camille's mission in Mexico. Play it wrong and not only would Thomas Dreyer likely demand their return to the U.S., as had been the original plan, but Aaron would jeopardize his future career.

At issue was Aaron's absolute certainty that Camille wouldn't leave Mexico without Rosalia Perez. And Aaron would never leave Camille to fight on her own. Short of being dragged away in a body bag, he'd have her back for as long as their mission took to complete—even if that meant disobeying a direct order from his superior.

He dialed Thomas Dreyer's personal number. He picked up on the second ring.

"Dreyer here."

"This is Montgomery."

"Did you and Fisher make it to La Paz?"

"We did, sir."

"Excellent. Arrangements have been confirmed for you two to hitch a ride to San Diego with a naval ship headed up the Pacific from South America."

Aaron screwed his mouth up. *Let the chess match begin.* "Fisher and I performed reconnaissance yesterday on the cartel compound where we were held. It had been vacated. We have no idea where Rosalia Perez was taken, sir."

Dreyer was silent for a beat. "Not surprising, given your escape. Not that the cartel is admitting to anything. They're demanding the prisoners' release in exchange for your freedom, and we've decided to let them go on believing they have the edge while we put the pieces in place for the girl's recovery. ICE received the San Diego

Police Department's blessing to handle the case, but our hands are tied at this point because the girl's citizenship has been brought into question. Mexican officials are pushing to handle the rescue themselves."

"Sounds like a political stunt."

"Roger that. If diplomacy fails, we've got a black ops team on standby in Mexico City."

"Who's leading the unit?" Aaron asked.

"Diego Santero."

Damn. He'd never met the guy in person, but by all accounts, he was a surly jackass of the first degree. Too bad he was also the best ICE black ops field agent in the world. When Aaron first set his sights on becoming a field agent, his motivation was to surpass the bar Santero had set.

He took a fortifying breath and hoped luck was on his side once more. Maybe he could turn his kidnapping into another golden ticket, one that led to his dream job with ICE. "If I can get a lead on Rosalia Perez's whereabouts, I want to be part of Santero's team for her extraction."

"Come again?"

"Officer Fisher and I are already in La Paz. We've had visual contact with Rosalia Perez and have a better chance than anyone of pinpointing where she's been taken. When I pass that intel on to ICE, I want to help with her rescue. I've trained for it—you know I have. I'm going to prove to you that I'm ICE agent material." He clamped his molars together, reeling at the note of desperation in his tone.

After a slow inhale, he tried again. "Think about it, sir. If Officer Fisher and I return to the States, we'll go into Witness Protection. We won't be doing anybody any good. If we stay in La Paz— where nobody, including the Mexican government, knows we are—we could make some real headway for ICE, not only with data on the cartel, but with a high-profile rescue. The intel I've already gathered about the cartel's smuggling operation alone will bump our unit to the best in the nation, guaranteed. This is our moment, sir. The opportunity our team's been waiting for." *That I've been waiting for.*

A long silence followed. "You're up for the challenge, Montgomery?"

"Absolutely."

"And Fisher, does she have the chops for this?"

"Fisher is former Special Forces. She was assigned to the Rosalia kidnapping case originally. With all due respect, sir, I don't think she'd leave Mexico without the girl if the President himself commanded her to."

Dreyer sighed and Aaron knew he'd won. "What do you need from me?"

"Time."

"Keep me in the loop, Montgomery. I'm putting my reputation on the line for you. Consider this your big audition. Don't screw it up."

"I won't, sir. Thank you."

After the call ended, Aaron sat for a long time, staring at his hands. The conversation had gone exactly as he'd hoped. Yet still, he couldn't shake the feeling that for the first time ever, his golden

ticket hadn't presented him with a great opportunity, but with a hangman's noose.

Aaron returned over an hour later, acting as
though nothing was amiss. Camille opened her
mouth to press him for details about where he'd
gone, but all that came out was a yawn.

"Let me show you your bed." Ana walked to the
sofa and removed its cushions. "My first apartment was a loft without enough space for both a
sofa and a bed, so my parents bought me this."

She tugged on a loop of material at the center
of the sofa and out popped a collapsible mattress.
The three of them made the bed with sheets and
a blanket.

Camille stroked the pillow nearest her. "I'm
tired just looking at it. I can't wait to sprawl."

Aaron raised an eyebrow. "On your side, of
course."

"What? You and I aren't sharing a bed."

He looked at her as though she was crazy. "We

escaped from a drug cartel and you're worried about sharing a bed with me?"

"Aaron, you're welcome to sleep with me," Ana purred. "My bed would accommodate both of us beautifully."

Camille huffed. "You're right, Aaron—I don't care what the sleeping arrangements are. Sleep with Ana or sleep on the sofa bed. Whatever."

Ana had that annoying smirk on her face again. "I'm going to retire to my room. If you two need anything, let me know."

Camille watched the bedroom door close behind Ana, then crawled between the sheets.

Aaron stood on the opposite side with his arms crossed over his chest, watching her. It was damned disconcerting. Ana had loaned her pajamas, but under Aaron's gaze, she felt positively naked. She snapped the sheet over herself, a warning for him to mind his p's and q's.

As though he'd been waiting for Camille's undivided attention, he squared his body to the bed and tugged his shirt over his head. As if he wanted

her to swoon over his rippling muscles and perfect physique.

Oh, please. What a jerk.

"I'm not sharing a bed with you if you're half-
naked." She tried to modulate her voice, but still,
it cracked once.

"We're going to be living in pretty close quarters for a while, so you'd better get used to the
sight of me." Grinning broadly, he dropped his
pants to the floor and stood with his hands on his
hip bones in a pair of flimsy red cotton boxer-
briefs.

Camille squeaked and scurried out of the bed.
"Jesus, Aaron, put your pants back on."

"Worried I'm going to attack you while you
sleep?"

"You already kissed me against my will. How
should I know what you're capable of?"

"I can say with one hundred percent certainty
that when we kissed, it was not against your will.
Look, I told you it wouldn't happen again and I'm

a man of my word. Any other promises you want me to make before we get in bed together?"

"Do you have to put it that way?"

"I think it has a nice ring to it."

"Promise you won't touch me."

He threw up his hands. "Oh, geez, Cam. I'm not a perv. I don't go around copping feels on frightened women."

"I'm not frightened." Especially not of some idiot who didn't have the decency to keep covered.

"Then why are you hiding behind that sheet?"

Camille looked to find her hands clutching the top sheet to her chest, nearly pulling it off the bed. She let go and straightened. She'd show him how not-frightened she was. "Say it."

Aaron yanked the sheets in his direction and fell into bed. The mattress groaned with the additional weight. "I promise not to grope you. Now stop yapping and get in bed."

With narrowed eyes, she lay back. She folded her hands over her stomach but found it uncomfortable, so she moved them to her sides. First above the covers, which was too chilly, and then below. She refluffed her pillow, flopped down and folded her hands across her chest. Aaron watched her with lazy eyes.

"How about I lie on my side and you can pretend I'm a wall?"

He turned his back to her and clicked off the floor lamp. Too much light streamed in from the streetlamp outside the window. Camille studied the taper of Aaron's wide shoulders to his trim waist. One thing was for sure—Aaron Montgomery could never be mistaken for a wall.

He knew Camille was tired. She'd gotten as little sleep as he had over the past few days. On the drive to La Paz, he'd seen the slump of her shoulders and the dark circles under her eyes. Yet Aaron felt those same eyes boring holes into his back long after he turned out the light.

After a while, Camille yawned quietly and shifted. Aaron squelched the urge to command

her to close her eyes. Instead, he tried a more dip-
lomatic approach.

"Camille, I can't get my mind to stop thinking
about kidnappings and guns and murder. Do you
mind if we talk a little to help me unwind?"

"Talk about what?"

He scrambled for a neutral topic. "What's your
favorite holiday?"

"Are you kidding?"

"No. It would be nice to think about something
happy."

She was quiet for so long that he didn't think
she'd answer. "Christmas," she blurted. "My favorite holiday is Christmas."

Aaron smiled, triumphant. "What makes it your
favorite?"

"My sister and Jacob stay overnight at our parents' house. I don't get to see Juliana much now
that she's married, so that's really nice. On Christmas morning, she does this big production of
handing out silly gifts that make us laugh."

He heard the joy in Camille's words and wanted

desperately to look at her but was afraid if he did, she'd clam up. "My mom makes this huge, elaborate meal and won't let us help. No matter what time she says dinner's at, it's always two hours late. Does your mom cook dinner?"

"We do it together. We make a turkey and a couple sides in the morning and nibble all day long. We never even sit at the dinner table. It's just… fun, relaxing. Next year'll be even better with little Alana for us to spoil."

Her voice drifted off. "Mmm," she added after a few quiet minutes.

It was a hum of contentment that rendered Aaron powerless to resist a peek. Careful not to shake the bed too much, he rolled over.

The light from the window slashed across the top of her head, illuminating her golden hair. She was asleep on her side facing him, with her hands on the pillow next to her cheek and a smile on her lips, totally peaceful.

Breathtaking.

He stared for a long time. She looked small,

angelic. This warrior who was so strong and capable, so ready to battle the world when she was awake, was still a woman when she slept. A beautiful, complicated woman.

He raised the sheet to cover her shoulder. Her nose wrinkled and he was tempted to kiss it until he remembered his promise. Well, Camille hadn't said anything about invading her personal space. Satisfied to have found a loophole, he moved his pillow to abut hers and nestled in. He covered her hand with his, curling his fingers until they reached her palm. With the steady rhythm of her breath on his cheek, Aaron closed his eyes and fell asleep.

Camille woke after dawn in Ana's sofa bed. Ready to fight the bad guys. One problem—she couldn't move.

Aaron had her pinned. He was asleep on his side, with his face so close that she had to pull back to keep from brushing his nose, and his arm and leg slung over her body.

"Aaron?" She pushed against his chest. "Aaron."

His eyes opened. "Good morning, Blondie."

She considered calling him on the use of that god-awful nickname, but first things first. "Get off me."

"I'm too comfortable to move."

"You promised not to touch me."

"I promised not to grope you. This is different. This is snuggling." He closed his eyes again.

"My foot's asleep and I have to use the bathroom. Get off or I'll make you."

"Fine," he said melodramatically.

Once free, Camille was flustered to discover that she, too, had been quite comfortable tangled up in bed with Aaron. She'd have to make sure it never happened again.

Sarah arrived less than an hour later to pick Ana up for work. Aaron locked the door after ushering the teachers out, then pulled two disposable cell phones from a paper bag. "I bought these last night and programmed each with three numbers—each other, Ana and Thomas Dreyer, my boss. I touched base with him last night and he's offering us ICE's full support."

"That's fantastic." She held out her hand for the phone, but he stared at her as if something was bothering him. "What?"

"I've got a really bad feeling about splitting up today. Maybe we should scrap the plan and stick together. You could come with me to find a place for us to stay and some wheels, and I could shop for supplies with you tonight."

Camille snatched the phone from his hand and pocketed it along with Ana's car keys. "Nothing's going to happen. The supermarket and clothing shops are only a mile or so away. Don't worry so much. I'm a cop, remember? You have to stop treating me like a civilian. Besides, the faster we get everything we need, the sooner we can get on with finding Rosalia."

Aaron took hold of Camille's elbows and looked so seriously into her eyes, the skin on the back of her neck tingled.

"We meet here tonight at five o'clock," he said.

"If something happens to me, if I don't come back, you call Dreyer. He'll get you out of Mexico by boat. The roads are too dangerous. There are armed checkpoints all along the highway to California. You don't want to get caught with a gun and you can't take the chance of coming across any crooked military types on the cartel's payroll. And don't try to be a hero by searching for Rosalia on your own. It's too risky. Promise me."

Rattled by his intensity, Camille whispered, "I promise."

"If something happens to you…if you're not back here tonight, I'll find you." He closed his eyes and screwed up his mouth. "Just be here. That's an order."

"I will. You, too, okay?" She pulled away from his grip. "At least you know I'm not leaving this neighborhood. I don't know where you're going to end up today."

"I don't know either. How about I call you at noon to check in?"

"All right. I'll be waiting." She gave him her best reassuring smile.

After donning a blue crocheted hat, she slipped a 9 mm into her waistband, then shoveled a few stacks of money into one pocket of her borrowed jacket and a backup handgun into another. She slipped on a pair of dark glasses and followed Aaron out the door.

Chapter 8

By eleven-thirty, Camille was half done with her errands. While the clothes she'd chosen for herself and Aaron weren't the most expensive or fashionable, they were good enough. She threw in some hats, socks and—despite her mortification at the idea—underwear for them both. Around the corner from the shoe store, she'd chucked the nasty cartel sneakers in a Dumpster with so much exuberance that a few heads turned to stare at her. She was feeling so good about her new footwear that, on a whim, she popped into a pharmacy for a new box of hair dye.

Brunette, just to tick Aaron off.

Back at the apartment, she scribbled a grocery list before heading out once more. Gigante Market, the local grocery chain, was as sprawling as an American supermarket, and she practically worked up a limp walking from the car to the main entrance.

Starting at the produce section, she methodically walked each aisle, adding to her cart. Inspired by the aroma of baking bread wafting from behind the bakery counter, she waited her turn for a loaf of fresh sweet bread. With an appreciative sigh, she popped a chunk of the still-warm loaf in her mouth, then got back to business. Rounding the corner to the rice aisle, she saw three men loitering at the opposite end, closest to the exit.

The pock-cheeked man who'd tied Aaron's and Camille's legs to those rusty patio chairs stood next to the man with helmet-hard hair who'd sky-dived with her and a third man Camille didn't recognize. He looked to be in his late thirties, with the muscular build of a bulldog. If any of the three could claim to be a full-time hit man for the cartel, it would be this guy.

Not sure if she was spotted, Camille flipped a U-turn and walked around the corner. She abandoned the shopping cart on the next aisle, slipped her firearm from her waist and flipped off the safety. She peeked between the shelves, through the bottles of juice on her side and the bags of rice on the other, at where the three men had been but were no longer.

They appeared quietly, with smirking, destructive smiles, at the head of the juice aisle.

Adrenaline and panic flamed to life within her, making her breath shallow, her vision narrow. Her gun hand shook violently.

The men advanced.

She swept an arm across a shelf of bottles, and they crashed to the ground, embedding little bits of glass into her ankles. She sprinted three aisles over, praying the glass and liquid impeded her pursuers long enough for her to make it out the front entrance.

Three against one in an aisle-by-aisle chase were terrible odds, though. Halfway through the snack aisle, Helmet Hair appeared before her. She squeezed a round off that went wide and then she turned back the way she came, but Hit Man and Pocked Face blocked her in. Their movement changing from running to stalking, they crowded in on her, drawing their guns.

She aimed her gun as best she could as it quaked in her hand and concentrated hard on her trigger finger, but it wouldn't move. Damn it.

On the edge of panic, she threw herself into a shelf, punching through the chips to the other side, and raced to the back of the store, scanning for a rear exit. What she came to first was the Mexican equivalent of an American deli section. She crashed into a refrigerated display case, then darted behind the counter and shoved past a shocked employee.

Dizzy with adrenaline and shock, she ducked behind a meat slicer and took in great gulps of air as blood surged with fiery purpose through her veins. Two sets of prowling feet appeared nearby. She tightened her grip on her gun as awareness dawned within her. She was going to have to kill them all if she wanted to make it out of the supermarket alive.

She rose into a squat beneath the table, waiting for the opportunity to strike.

Her cell phone rang.

She cursed and leaped from her hiding place. Helmet Hair, with his back to her, was the closest. Cringing with the effort of squeezing the trigger, she got a round off, hitting him in the shoulder. She kicked out at his midsection, knocking him face-first into the revolving vertical meat broiler. He shrieked in pain.

She twisted left and shot Pocked Face in the gut. He staggered and leveled his pistol at her.

Dodging right, she fired again, the bullet slicing a chunk from his neck. Blood gushed uncontrollably from both wounds. With a guttural cry, he shot at her at the same time Hit Man caught her left cheek with an upper jab.

The impact of the punch knocked her down. She rolled under the nearest stainless-steel table. Pocked Face fired in her direction and the table rocked on its legs as the bullet ricocheted and hit a display case, shattering glass in all directions. She braced for a second shot but none came. The only sound besides Helmet Hair's low moans of agony from the meat broiler was the soft clunk of Pocked Face's head hitting the floor.

Hit Man's booted feet moved toward her.

Gripping her gun hand hard with her left to minimize the quaking, she squeezed the trigger and got a shot off. It went wide.

She squeezed again.

The gun clicked benignly. Out of ammo.

She unzipped her jacket's inside pocket and reached for her backup weapon, but it snagged on the pocket liner.

Another spray of bullets rocked the table. Her time was running out. She fumbled with the jacket pocket but couldn't control her fingers enough to untangle the gun. Adrenaline and fear were making her clumsier with every passing second. With her pulse whooshing in her ears, she scrambled out the other end of the table.

Keeping low, she slipped back into the public area of the now-deserted store. The gunfire had done an effective job of clearing out shoppers. She dashed past the milk refrigerators toward the bakery, fumbling in her jacket pocket as she moved.

She veered behind the bakery display counter and hurled herself to the ground. Her hand shook so hard she couldn't close her fingers over the gun, much less unsnag it from the pocket lining and bring it out. She ground her teeth with rage against her stupid limitations that were about to get her killed. Taking a second deep breath, she focused on steadying her hand, but it was too late.

Hit Man dragged her up and punched her square in the cheek he'd already pummeled. This time, Camille hit back. She put all her weight behind a right uppercut to his chin and when she retracted her fist, she backhanded the other side of his face.

He grabbed hold of her left wrist and torqued

it until she screamed. She was millimeters away from having her arm broken and so she pivoted, desperate to straighten her arm. As soon as her back was to him, he released her wrist and locked his arm around her neck in a stranglehold.

She gasped for air that would not come. He tightened his grip and the edges of her vision went black. Struggling against an onslaught of shock, she shoved her quaking hand inside the pocket of her jacket, threaded the gun under her armpit and clamped down with her arm to steady her grip.

She fired twice.

Hit Man slumped over her. The unnatural warmth of spilled blood pooled across her back. Shouldering him off, she left the gun in her now-ragged jacket and ran out the screen door at the rear of the bakery, into an alley.

She paused and did a quick assessment of herself. Her side ached, probably from bullet shrapnel, she had a mean shiner on her cheek and she was covered in blood. It saturated her jacket, splattered into her hair and ran down her arms and legs.

Her cell phone rang again, a confusingly normal sound that blended with the wailing of multiple police sirens closing in. She wouldn't answer Aaron's call because no matter what she said, the fear and adrenaline in her voice would come through and she couldn't take the chance that he'd come for her. She'd rather die before dragging him into this new danger. Until she could guarantee Aaron's safety, she'd have to make due on her own.

She fished out the phone, turned the ringer off and ran.

She ran as fast and as long as her leg and its debilitating pain allowed. Then she kept going anyway, more slowly, but still making progress. Keeping to alleyways, trash heaps and abandoned buildings, she shrank into the shadows of the city and disappeared.

A tingling of dread niggled at Aaron when Camille didn't answer her phone. He called her at noon like he'd promised and again a few minutes later, but it rang and rang. After that, the phone was answered by a computerized message. Either her phone had been switched off or destroyed. Any way he looked at it, something was wrong.

His simmering dread devolved into full-fledged panic when, at three o'clock, he stopped by Ana's apartment and Camille was not there. Bags of new clothes had been piled on the sofa, but no Camille. He jogged to the supermarket where she'd planned to shop.

At the edge of the supermarket parking lot, he dropped to his knees at the sight of three covered bodies being loaded into ambulances. The parking lot was nearly empty of civilian vehicles and it didn't take any time at all to locate Ana's car.

Crazy with fear, he raced back to Ana's apartment to wait for her to come home from work so he could enlist her help. The market was crawling with cops and no way could Aaron take the chance of being recognized. If Camille was alive, what good would he be to her if he were taken into custody? Ana was already home when he arrived and agreed to go to the market to ask witnesses about the identities of the dead. Or, at least, if any of the bodies were an American female.

Dear God, let her be alive.

Aaron kept vigil at the apartment, holding on to hope Camille would show up at five o'clock as they'd agreed. He cleaned and reloaded his guns twice, checked the strength of his phone service every minute or two and paced in circles around the kitchen table. He put in a call to Nicholas Wells, his task-force buddy, but word of the market shoot-out hadn't trickled Stateside.

Five o'clock came and went.

Ana returned at five-thirty, frustrated by the lack of information she'd been able to elicit from onlookers. All she learned was that the market was a wreck, with blood and knives and bullets everywhere.

Together they waited thirty minutes more, until Aaron could no longer bear the idleness. After scribbling his cell phone number, he grabbed the bags of clothing and their stash of weapons, slung them around his body and loped to the dirt bike he'd purchased that morning. The heavy load was awkward and took a lot of concentration to balance, but he was grateful for the distraction to keep his mind from hurtling off the deep end.

After dropping the clothes and guns off at their new hideout, he sat on the bike on the side of the road, fingering his phone. If he didn't hear from her by midnight, he'd call Dreyer and enlist Santero's help. His terror at Camille's fate was palpable—like a second person standing too close, whispering, *I told you it was a bad idea to split up* over and over into his ear. Every five minutes, he redialed her number.

He decided not to search for her. It was a strange city, so large that the futility of a search was bound to destroy whatever hope he had left. And he might not hear her call over the high-pitched whine of the bike's engine.

At nine o'clock, after nine full hours of experiencing a level of panic he hadn't known was possible to survive from, his phone rang.

"Aaron?" Camille's voice was weak and breathy.

Aaron gritted his teeth against the emotion welling in his throat. She was alive.

"You scared me." His choked whisper sounded oddly similar to hers. "What took you so long to call?"

"I think I passed out."

Aaron closed his eyes. Now was not the time to lose the careful control he'd clung to all day. "Tell me where you are and I'll come get you."

She directed him to a partially constructed cinder-block structure in an alley off a major thoroughfare and asked him to bring her a change of clothes. She swore to him she'd keep her phone close at hand while she waited. Still, he hated the uncertainty that came with hanging up the call.

He flew through the streets in a daze and stopped next to a darkened cinder-block shell of a house, disbelieving that his Camille was inside such a cruel, filthy place. He'd never let a woman he knew walk through this alley, let alone linger after dark with only rats, roaches and stray dogs as company.

Camille sat in the far corner of the structure, propped against the wall. The bright lights of the thoroughfare streamed in through the empty spaces that would have been windows if the house had been finished. It was enough light to see Camille's swollen face and the dried brown blood that coated her like paint.

He ran to her and dropped to the ground.

"Where are you hurt?" He ripped the blood-drenched jacket and shirt over her head. "Where are you hurt, goddamn it?"

"It's not my blood."

He smoothed his fingers over her back, inspecting her skin, slick with blood and sweat, for the wound that was most certainly there. The jacket bore the irrefutable evidence of a bullet hole and a life-threatening wound.

"Where were you hit, Cam? Talk to me." His voice was frantic as his hands finished with her back and started on her front, roving over her stomach and sides and arms.

"It's not my blood."

"Like hell it's not. There's too much of it."

With a violent yank of material, her bloody, tattered pants were off. His hands grazed the lengths of her legs. Bits of glass were embedded in her calves, but that wasn't what he was looking for.

"Aaron, stop. It's not my blood. I swear."

Finally, with no inch of her body left unchecked, he stood. His pulse was racing, his breath coming in ragged fits. Impossible that she could be covered in so much blood and not be injured. *Impossible.* But whatever her wounds were, he had to get a grip before he got them into more trouble.

He had to get Camille to safety. The urge to protect her was fierce. At that moment, there were fifty-fifty odds he'd call Dreyer to get them out of the country by morning. They might have to hide for the rest of their lives in WitSec, but she'd be safe and that was all that mattered.

He looked her way. Wearing nothing but panties and a bra, she sat utterly still, chanting quietly, looking more fragile than he knew her capable of being. That certainly got his attention.

Finally, he heard what she was chanting.

"It's not my blood."

Blinking rapidly, he nodded, processing. "It's not your blood."

"No."

"Whose?"

"Two men from the compound and another I didn't recognize."

"You killed them?"

"Yeah," she said wearily.

"You weren't shot?"

"No, just a little beat up."

Aaron looked around the ground for the change of clothes he'd brought, that he'd dropped in a fit of panic when he'd seen her. "Here, hurry. We need to leave."

She put her clothes on while sitting, even her pants. Aaron couldn't tear his eyes away from her, as if his sight held the power to keep her from evaporating into thin air. When she was done, he handed her a helmet.

"A motorcycle?"

"Dirt bike. With helmets on, there's no chance of being recognized."

Camille nodded. Aaron offered her a hand, which she accepted. She grimaced as she pushed to her feet, as though she was injured worse than the superficial wound on her ankle. But he had inspected every inch of her body.

"What's wrong?"

"Nothing," she replied thickly. "Get the bike started. I'll be out in a sec."

"No. You're not getting out of my sight again."

"I'm right behind you."

"What are you hiding from me, Camille?"

"I need a minute."

Then he noticed the way she stood—on her right foot. The pieces fell into place. The grocery store was at least six or seven miles away.

"You ran, didn't you? From the market?"

"I did what I had to do. Please, wait at the bike. I'll be there in a sec."

Aaron lifted her into his arms. Her bad leg had to be killing her, and she didn't want him to see her limp. Stubborn, stubborn woman.

"You promised—no pity."

"Right. No pity," he murmured absentmindedly as he walked.

"Then what do you call this?"

Taking care of you, my proud warrior. "Only trying to speed things along."

They barreled through the city. The feel of Camille, with her arms holding tight around his middle and her warmth pressed against his back, was a balm against the fear and regret that had consumed him. She was alive, relatively uninjured and safe.

Pulling into a private marina, Aaron cut the engine on the bike and used his feet to walk them down the ramp to the dock.

"You bought us a yacht?"

"Yeah." He helped her from the bike and over

the railing of the boat. "Transportation-slash-housing all rolled into one."

Camille nodded. She looked exhausted.

He lifted the bike over the rail and onto the deck of the boat. Its lightness was one of the main reasons Aaron bought a dirt bike instead of a motorcycle. The other was its ability to traverse both streets and off-road trails, wherever their search for Rosalia Perez took them.

"The bathroom's by the bed," he said. "I'm going to get us offshore, then we'll talk."

"Okay." But she didn't move, just stood on her right leg, probably waiting for him to turn away so he wouldn't see her limp. Stubborn woman. Though he wanted to carry her, her safety was more important. Every moment on land kept Camille in danger.

Aaron untied the ropes that anchored them to the dock and climbed the ladder to the bridge. With a turn of a key, the boat rumbled to life. He pushed the throttle forward and the boat responded, racing them into the safety of the deep, black sea.

One hour later, with the boat anchored in a leeward cove of a tiny island off the coast, he sat on the bed and waited for Camille to finish showering, holding a pair of scissors and a box of hair dye he'd found amid her purchases. He worshipped her hair but valued her life even more. Maybe if she'd disguised her appearance sooner, before Aaron stopped her, the shoot-out could've been avoided. He wouldn't make such a careless mistake again.

She emerged from the bathroom dressed in sweatpants and a white T-shirt. The bruises on her cheek looked even worse in the light. Her left eye was almost completely swollen shut, but she zeroed in on the items in his hands and nodded.

She took a step and sniffed. Gathering her in his arms, he ignored her weak protestations and deposited her on the toilet lid.

Without a word, she turned, offering him access to her hair. He gathered it in his hand, gave it one final caress.

"I'm so sorry," he whispered. Then he made the first cut.

Before long, blond locks littered the floor. Camille remained still and silent as Aaron snipped her hair to chin length. When he'd finished, he opened the box of dye.

"I don't know how…" he started.

She turned toward him and set her hand over his. "I'll help you."

Her fingers were cold, shaky. He dropped to his knees and brought her hand to his lips. He felt a welling of sorrow and anger stir within him, threatening his careful composure, and cleared his throat. "We'll save enough dye for my hair, too. We're in this together."

She nodded and took the box of dye. Bent over the instructions together, they got to work.

An hour later, they were brunettes. Aaron dabbed her hair one final time with a towel, then lifted her into his arms. She complied without complaint as he carried her to the bed.

Rolling to her side, she stared at the wall with stormy intensity.

After turning off the lights, Aaron stripped to his boxers and slid beneath the covers, all the way over to her. She didn't acknowledge his nearness, but she didn't protest either. He rested the entire length of his body along her back, spooning her tightly. His fingers locked with hers.

He spent nine hours that day thinking she'd died in a vicious gun battle. Though he knew better now, he felt damaged by the experience. Tonight, he needed to hold her as much for his own healing as for hers.

Tonight, she let him.

Chapter 9

Camille woke with Aaron's nose touching her cheek and his arm draped across the underside of her breasts. She should get up. They had so much to do. Every moment they wasted kept their families and Rosalia in danger. But his body felt heavy and good and she dreaded moving her throbbing left leg.

She worked her fingers through the tips of Aaron's thick hair and felt the ends where it curled around his ear. He looked as handsome as ever with brown hair. Her fingers glided over his earlobe and around the strong angle of his jaw. When she did not dare explore him further, she rested the palm of her hand against his neck and concentrated on the beat of his pulse.

It would be worse now for her. If they survived this mission, it would be painful in a way she wanted to deny but couldn't—not if she was being honest with herself. She'd invested years of her energy hating Aaron, on actively trying not to think about what she wanted from him. That would be impossible now. The man she held for this brief moment in time beneath the palm of her hand would exist forever on the fringe of her life, unattainable and heartbreaking. She should have tried harder to hate him.

When the tickle of blinking eyelashes brushed her cheek, her hand flew from Aaron's neck. Silently, he levered himself onto an elbow. She met his fathomless brown eyes, felt his arms slide along her shoulders, caging her beneath him, his fingers tangling in her hair. He lowered his mouth. Through no conscious will of her own, Camille's lips parted. Hovering only centimeters above her, he closed his eyes, his breathing strained, shallow.

A lock of his hair fell forward, skimming her forehead. She closed her eyes, the effort to stay still, to not pull his head down that final bit, sapping her already negligible strength.

He sucked in a deep, tremulous gulp of air, rolled off the bed and staggered to the bathroom. Camille let go of the sheet she was twisting and pushed to a seated position at the edge of the bed. Her whole body hurt, as if the pain of her leg had seeped into her bloodstream and spread while she slept.

Good. Anything to keep her mind from dwelling on what just happened.

When Aaron emerged from the bathroom, neither spoke as he carried her up the three stairs to the sofa. She let him because, frankly, she couldn't think of a damn thing to say.

"This is the living area," he said without meeting her eyes. "There's a deck out back with a ladder that leads to the bridge. The boat's only thirty-three feet long, which is tiny, I know, but it was the best I could do."

In addition to the sofa on which Camille sat, the main cabin housed a dining table and a kitchenette complete with a sink, mini-fridge and microwave. "Actually, it's not much smaller than my apartment. How much did you pay?"

"A hundred grand, which would be steep for a legitimate sale of a yacht this size, but on the black market, it seemed a reasonable price, especially since the guy selling it didn't care who I was and why I had so much cash. He got the boat as a gift for his wife last year and now she's hinting about a bigger one. Must be nice."

"This is perfect. Really great thinking." She tried to smile, but the action brought too much pain to her swollen cheek. "I didn't know you had experience with boats."

He shrugged. "Yeah. I've done my share of water-skiing and speedboating over the years. Never captained a yacht, but I'm getting the hang of it."

"How far offshore are we?"

He emptied a can of soup into a coffee mug. "Twenty miles. About an hour's drive."

"Great. I'll heat up the soup. You fire up the boat. We can start with surveillance. Make a few passes by the Gigante Market, see if any other cartel operators are lurking nearby who might lead us to Rosalia."

He set the mug in the microwave. "We're going to shore this afternoon, but only to meet Ana at the marina. She called last night while you were showering to check on you and offered to drop off some groceries. I asked her to pick up the package from Jacob and some materials one of my co-workers overnighted to me, too. You'll be staying in the cabin, out of sight. You're not getting off this boat for a few more days."

Anger tightened her throat. "Who the hell are you to issue a command like that? If I say I'm all right—" She pushed to standing, swallowing a gasp as waves of pain radiated from her leg.

Aaron was in her face before she could recover enough to speak, stabbing the air between them with his finger. His eyes were wild, furious. "Sit down. Right now. Never once in my life have I forced a woman to do anything she didn't want to, but so help me, Camille, you're going to stay off that leg if I have to tie you to the bed."

Camille bit back the challenge hanging on the tip of her tongue. *I'd like to see you try.* Because what if he seized on her words? What if he touched her again?

Still, she was far too stubborn to capitulate. Balancing on her good leg, she held her ground. "How dare you, you chauvinistic jackass. You'd never talk to one of your ICE unit members like that. If I say I'm all right, then I am. The fact that I'm a woman is immaterial."

Yet how could she ignore that truth when he stood so close? When she could smell soap on his skin and watch the throb of a vein in his forehead? She'd never been more aware that she was a woman than when she was near Aaron Montgomery. And for that alone, she wished she could hate him.

"You're a terrible patient."

"And you're an insufferable pig."

She jumped a little when she felt his hand on her hip. Trapped between his broad, solid body and the sofa, her only move was to scramble onto the cushions, but she was too confused to move. She sought out an answer in his eyes and found them narrowed with resolve.

"You're right. Your gender doesn't matter to me one bit. Never has, never will." His voice had turned a soothing, patronizing tone. His hand, rough and sure, slid along her thigh and she caught herself pressing into his touch as her body stirred to life. "In fact, I barely notice you're a woman at all." His other hand closed around her waist as his fingers skimmed her knee.

Her breathing grew shallow. She stared at his chest, unwilling to meet his gaze.

"But if we got in a jam while doing surveillance, you couldn't run fast enough to escape." He dug his fingertips into the sensitive hollow behind her knee and her standing leg buckled. Her arms flailed as she dropped to the sofa. "And if you were caught, what good would you be to Rosalia?"

He was right, damn him.

She stared out the window at the rolling gray swells, her hands fisted to keep herself from rubbing the skin he'd seared with his touch. She could think of nothing to say, no clever retort or convincing threat. No argument to match his foolproof logic. She had to let him win this one. For Rosalia. For their families.

He banged the mug of soup down on the side table. She lifted it to her lips and drank deeply. Through her silence, she conceded defeat.

For the rest of the day, the yacht bobbed in the Sea of Cortez, so far from the mainland it looked like a layer of brown smog across the western horizon. Outside of using the bathroom, Aaron let Camille do nothing for herself—not walk, get a drink of water or brush her hair. He hovered, like the world's most handsome private nurse, over her every waking moment.

At four o'clock, the yacht rumbled to life and they made their way through the long, narrow Bay of La Paz. When they reached their slip in the marina, Aaron ducked his head into the cabin with a warning for Camille to stay out of sight. She responded with a huff of protest. After resting her knee for a full night and day, she was anxious to measure her recovery.

She waited for the sound of Aaron's heavy footfalls on the dock, listening to men calling out to each other in Spanish, car horns honking in the distance and the cries of seagulls, then eased onto her feet.

"Ugh, that smarts," she muttered under her breath as her every nerve ending protested the move. Using the cabin wall as a crutch, she limped toward the door and into the sunlight.

Ana was waiting for them outside the locked security gate at the top of the ramp with four grocery bags, watching Aaron with a seductive grin as he approached. When she noticed Camille, she waved and her smile turned cheerful. Aaron glanced over his shoulder, then unlocked the gate for Ana. After grabbing the grocery bags, he stalked back down the ramp.

"What do you think you're doing?"

Camille clamored over the boat railing and onto the dock, schooling a grimace of discomfort away from her features. Standing on one leg as she was, she looked like a flamingo, but she refused to play into Aaron's argument by leaning on the boat for support. "Saying hello to Ana. You got a problem with that?"

"It's not safe out here. What if someone recognizes you?"

"What if someone recognizes *you?*"

His face reddened with fury. "I'm not the one—"

"Camille, I've been so worried!" Ana skirted Aaron to kiss Camille's cheek and pet her head. "Your hair looks beautiful in this shade. How are you?"

Camille leveled a defiant glare on Aaron before turning her attention to Ana.

"I'm fine. All I needed was a bit of rest."

Aaron scoffed.

Ana squeezed Camille's hand. "The rumor has always been that the cartel's control was limited to the commercial port near the ferry landing. If I had any idea the grocery store would be dangerous, I never would have suggested you shop there."

Aaron moved next to Camille and took her elbow in his hand. She tugged out of his grip. He draped an arm around her rib cage and pulled her tightly against his side. "Hopefully, with the intelligence Camille and I gather, we can help end the cartel's stronghold on your city. Getting back to something you mentioned—the rumor is that the cartel controls the commercial port?"

"That's what I've heard."

Aaron rubbed his jaw. "That might be useful."

"Whatever I can do to help."

"You've already helped," Camille said. "Thank you for bringing us food. I've never been so hungry in my life."

Aaron released her to rummage through the bags. He handed her a banana, the peel already started. As if she couldn't have done that herself. The man needed to chill out before she strangled him.

"Sorry for the brief visit, but we need to shove off. Too risky to linger." He stowed the grocery bags on deck, then took Ana's arm and speared a finger in Camille's direction. "I'm walking Ana up the dock. You don't move. I'll help you in the boat when I get back. No argument."

Yeah, right.

She hobbled along the side of the boat and took her first good look at it. It appeared smaller from the outside and practically brand-new. The metal shone, the windows were clean, the white hull was free of blemishes.

Then she noticed the boat's name. Raising her eyebrows, she stared in disbelief at the hot pink lettering. She read the words silently, then aloud, then silently again. Her laughter erupted first as a chortle deep in her lungs and rapidly devolved into waves of giggles with a touch of crazy thrown in—the kind of laughter she rarely, if ever, indulged in.

She couldn't help it.

Tears pooled in the corners of her eyes and her nose started to run. She laughed so hard that it soon made no sound, taking the form of silent full-body shudders that made her stomach muscles ache. She doubled over, bracing a hand on her good leg. She laughed so hard, she nearly forgot about her pain.

Aaron jogged into view. "What's wrong?"

He sounded worried, so she waved dismissively at him. He set his hands on her shoulders. "Camille, are you laughing or crying?"

The concern in his voice made her laugh harder. She pointed a shaky finger at the boat.

"Oh, that." Aaron was smiling now, too. "Perfect name, isn't it? Kind of sums up our whole experience."

It took a few throat clearings before Camille could speak. "I have never, ever seen something so inappropriately named...and in hot pink to boot. It's like a floating joke. Who names their boat *that?*"

"An optimist?"

Well, that was about the funniest thing Aaron could have said. Camille's face contorted as she fell into another onslaught of unfettered giggles. Aaron pulled her into an easy embrace and she was too distracted by her giddiness to push him away. They rested their foreheads on each other's shoulders and let laughter overtake them.

When they were all laughed out, they broke apart and mopped their faces. Camille watched Aaron untie the boat from the dock. Then he lifted her into his arms and carried her on board the *Happily Ever After.*

Aaron pulled the boat away from the private marina slip that the previous owner had prepaid a year's rent for. It was a load off his mind to have a secure place to dock. Now he only had to worry about the minor detail of Camille's safety, he thought with halfhearted sarcasm, knowing how oppressively it weighed on his conscience.

As he rounded the jetty separating the marina from the rest of the bay, an expensive-looking powerboat cut in front of the yacht. The four men on board didn't fit. They neither looked wealthy, nor out for a pleasure cruise of the bay. As he considered them, all men on board except the captain drew guns.

Cursing, he wrenched the steering wheel to the left and maxed the throttle. With a great rumbling, the yacht accelerated, but it was not a craft built for speed or tight maneuverability. Though he pushed their lumbering floating house to its max speed in the glassy water, the powerboat easily caught up.

"What're you doing?" Camille called behind him.

"They found us. Get your gun."

Side by side, the boats flew toward the mouth of the bay, dodging sailboats and fishing boats, buoys and kayaks.

Camille appeared again, armed with a rifle. She held up a grenade. "Get us in a position to use it."

While Aaron negotiated the bay, she crouched along the side wall of the bridge and shot a dozen or so rounds at the powerboat. She ducked as their weapons fired in response, then peered back over the edge.

"They're trying to board our boat," she yelled, squeezing off another volley of rounds. Bits of fiberglass rained on Aaron as the men returned fire.

Outrunning the powerboat was impossible. If they were going to survive, Aaron had to be smarter than the men trying to overtake them. In the distance, a beastly freighter laden with huge red-and-yellow shipping containers surged through the water.

"Keep them off our boat," he called to Camille. "I have a plan."

"Got it." She tipped her rifle over the railing and fired.

Aaron angled the yacht straight at the freighter's bow in a deadly game of chicken. As he knew it would, the powerboat corrected its angle to match the yacht. Neck and neck, they careened toward the freighter with alarming speed.

When they were within a few hundred yards of the container ship, he shouted, "Get ready to throw that grenade."

One at a time, Aaron wiped his sweaty palms on his jeans. He was an inexperienced boat captain and this next move would be a feat of boating expertise if he pulled it off. If he didn't, he and Camille were about to smash headfirst into a shipping barge.

"Ready, Cam?"

"Ready."

Fifty feet to impact. Forty. The barge's horn blasted a warning.

Thirty feet. Fifteen.

"Now! Now!"

He couldn't look to see if Camille threw the grenade, or if it reached its target. The powerboat peeled off to the left side of the freighter as Aaron wrenched the wheel to the right, close enough to the ship to see the gray-green barnacles on its hull.

The yacht lurched and bucked in the wake of the freighter as a loud explosion boomed all around them. Black smoke curled into the sky from the other side of the ship. Camille hit her mark. As he raced for the open ocean, Aaron glanced over his shoulder at the skeleton of the speedboat, spewing fire and sinking into the bay.

Fury uncoiled in his gut. Every move they made, someone got the jump on them. Well, no more. Aaron's tolerance for playing defense had reached its threshold. How could they rescue a child when they could barely survive a grocery run to shore? How would they ever be free with a faceless enemy anticipating their every move and making the first strike?

Camille flopped into the cocaptain's chair. "It's like they were waiting for me at the Gigante Market. And now this. It can't be a coincidence." She sat a little straighter. "Ana…"

"Maybe. For all we know, the guy who sold me

the boat tipped off the cartel about his slip in the marina. Or there's a rat on the task force leaking information. Anything's possible. From now on, we don't trust anyone—not ICE, not the SDPD, not Ana. We've got each other, Cam, and that's it."

After anchoring the yacht in the lee of one of the numerous uninhabited islands offshore, Aaron opened the package from Nicholas Wells. At the dining table, he and Camille leafed through a gray binder outlining the top operatives of the Cortez Cartel's weapon-smuggling unit, complete with names, aliases and photos.

Now that they'd decided not to trust Ana, Aaron was prepared to disregard her tip about the cartel's operations in La Paz's commercial port, but Wells seconded the intel in a handwritten note he'd included in the package. He and Camille would need to watch their backs and go in heavily armed, but the lead was too significant to ignore.

He watched Camille study the folder, her sharp gaze taking in the data with the practiced eye of a cop and a keen intelligence that never ceased to awe him, her slender fingers skimming the photographs. Her thick, brown hair fell like a curtain between them. It would be so easy to rake his fingers through it and tip her head back to expose the delicate length of her throat. He would taste her. He would drink his fill. And maybe those fingers would wrap around his shoulders and cling to him.

He wanted her to cling to him. And not just with those perfect fingers, but with her whole self. Someday soon, he vowed. He would have her in his arms, in their bed, for as long as he wanted, without the pressure of survival hanging over them. He shook his head, floored by the direction of his thoughts. Never in a million years would he have imagined he'd wish for more time with Camille Fisher, of all people.

All he knew was that sometime since they'd been taken to Mexico, his feelings for her had shifted in a catastrophic way. What he planned to do about it, he had no idea. For now, his only plan was keeping them alive and finding Rosalia Perez. He'd worry about the rest later.

"This guy, Eduardo Vasillo," she said, tapping a photograph. "He's one of the men who attacked me in the market."

He forced his mind to stay focused on the photograph—not Camille's fingers or hair.

"Sal de Largo," she went on, pointing to another picture on the page. "He was one of my attackers, too."

Aaron slipped the photographs from their pockets and crumpled them up. "We don't have to worry about them anymore. Let's see if anyone else looks familiar."

She turned the page. With how fast everything had happened in the past few days, the details of their captors' appearances were fuzzy in their memories. Every face, that was, except El Ocho, Rodrigo Perez, whose image Aaron recognized from the photograph Dreyer shared at his last taskforce meeting. Perez wasn't the cartel boss, that was Alejandro Milán, but trapping Milán was virtually impossible, as the man was a ghost. If it could have been done, then either the Mexican government would have arrested him or a rival cartel would have killed him already.

The wheels were turning in Aaron's head. Sick of playing defense, he was hungry for battle. He was going to personally rescue Rosalia and take down Rodrigo Perez. And once Perez's minions were good and confused, they would scatter, and Aaron and Camille would be free.

Chapter 10

There days later, Aaron woke before dawn. His erection was painful this time, throbbing with awareness of the woman sleeping mere inches away. He palmed it. It was hard as steel beneath his fingers. He could slip away to the bathroom for some temporary relief, but any cure he administered would be fleeting at best. After all, when he was done, he'd return to bed and it would start all over again. He let go and propped his hands behind his head.

Time to embrace the pain.

He wanted her badly. Every day, every night. It wasn't only her strength or her mouthwatering body that drew him to her, but every single damn thing about her, good and bad, pleasant and unpleasant. Everything.

The prosaic hours of her recovery had left Aaron with nothing to do but concentrate on her. Even his dreams wouldn't grant him a reprieve. Tonight's dream had been achingly vivid. Truth was, he was starting to hate the bed they shared. Because every night, she was there—close enough to touch, yet with such a wall of ice around her heart that breaching it seemed impossible.

The worst part was he felt possessive of her in a primitive way—which was royally disturbing for a modern, pro-feminist guy like he thought he was. The feeling had built to the point that he caught himself thinking he *owned* her body, proudly assessing and cataloging her attributes in his mind. From the mole on the top of her right foot to her slender fingers to the baby-fine hair at her neck, with each new detail he discovered, he simply thought, *that's mine.*

Her fleeting moments of vulnerability especially

belonged to him. He'd seen her scared and sleepy, nervous and in pain, both furious and in the throes of uncontrollable giggles. These glimpses of her soul filled him with the kind of puffed-up machismo that declared *no other man knows her this way, only me.* And wasn't that a disquieting thought?

Holding her while they slept had devolved into yet another primordial demonstration of his ownership—as if, as a holdover of some ancient instinct passed down through thousands of years of male genes, he was protecting what was his. She was turning him into a caveman.

And she couldn't be more indifferent to him. She was impervious to flattery, chivalry, humor and all other types of flirting. He had to find a way to break the ice wall because his tolerance for her disinterest had reached its threshold. With the way they were risking their lives, he'd be damned if he spent many more nights trapped in another kind of torture. She was his and it was time she figured it out.

He just needed a better strategy.

Camille's bottom rustled against his thigh, the feel of which was both torturous and, though he fought hard to deny it, as necessary as breathing. Letting out a frustrated snort, he pulled her more snugly against him and stroked the fabric of her pajamas absentmindedly.

Maybe he'd been too subtle. Whenever she was nervous or scared, he backed off to a safe distance. In retrospect, that was probably the worst thing he could have done. He'd given her too much space to deny what she felt, too much leeway to ignore their mutual attraction. It was time to drop the metaphorical hammer on her head.

He plodded from the room and climbed to the bridge, inhaling the crisp ocean air. Four days had passed since the Gigante Market shoot-out. Despite his dread at the notion, he could no longer justify bobbing in the lee of an uninhabited island for the sake of Camille's recovery. She no longer walked with a limp and the bruise on her cheek had subsided to a faint discoloration. It was time to return to shore and to the mission that threatened their lives at every turn.

After raising the anchor, he brought the boat to life and started the tedious drive through the bay to scope out a new marina slip to rent, paid for in cash under an alias. All the while, his mind remained fixed on the woman sleeping a few feet beneath him, plotting the details of her seduction.

La Paz had a large selection of private marinas for Aaron and Camille to choose from. They settled on one far enough from the commercial port to offer them a buffer should the cartel run periodic security sweeps around the vicinity of the port, but near enough to the main road that they could dock and set off on dirt bike if they caught a new lead.

Once docked, they zipped into town on their bike to pick up a can of white paint from a small hardware store. The flamboyant yacht name had given them a good laugh, but hot pink lettering and covert ops didn't jibe together. If Aaron and

Camille wanted to stay alive and conduct a rescue, they needed to be as invisible as they could.

That accomplished, Camille sat on the bridge with Aaron as he braved the open water of the bay to reposition them as near to the commercial port as possible without arousing the suspicion of the police boats cruising the harbor or the machine gun-toting guards lining the dock terminal.

Maybe such tight security was standard, but Camille doubted it. "Guess the local law enforcement noticed our boat chase. We'll have to be even more careful not to get spotted. Going to Mexican jail would cramp my style."

"That makes two of us. I'll keep our boat inconspicuous. You get in the cabin and start looking for familiar faces or anything suspicious on the dock. The sooner we figure out if the cartel is operating out of the port, the sooner we can get the hell out of the line of fire."

Pichilingue, the so-named location of the commercial port and ferry landing, was really a short strip of land that jutted, hooklike, into the bay, creating a small, vegetation-free cove polluted with litter and oily water, overburdened with tall cranes and concrete piers. Presently commanding the focus of the dock workers and cranes was a huge ferry with peeling white paint and faded red lettering on the side reading *Puerto Azul.* The back end of the ferry had been lowered to form a ramp for the waiting semitrucks, car freighters and civilian vehicles to drive on board.

Camille sat in the cabin with the gray binder on her lap and a pair of binoculars in hand, but even after two hours of looking, the stakeout hadn't yielded any results. Aaron had tucked the boat into the shadow of an anchored sportfishing boat, which seemed to be keeping their profile low enough to escape notice.

Rapidly running out of patience, she repositioned to the rear of the cabin and shifted her focus away from the port, to the buildings beyond the dock fence line.

Bingo.

Within the jumble of warehouse buildings, at an

angle that hadn't been visible before, two men in dark gray blazers and black jeans paced between a shiny black sedan and a heavily graffitied building lined with roll-up metal doors. Clearly, they were either waiting for something to happen or trying to make sure nothing did. Though neither displayed an obvious weapon, their stiff postures and shifty gazes spoke loud and clear of their capacity for menace.

She flipped through the folder from the ICE task force, comparing the men at the warehouse to the photos of the known cartel members.

She struck gold.

"Hello there, Carlos 'Two Down' Reyes," she muttered. Why he went by Two Down was an answer she hoped to never learn.

Tossing the binder aside, she pushed open the cabin door and opened her mouth to holler at Aaron about her discovery. But before she could speak, the yacht rumbled to life and started to move. Camille braced a hand on the bridge ladder as the boat picked up speed and flipped a U-turn.

"Hey, Aaron, what's happening?"

"Think we've been made by the harbor police."

Camille whirled around. Sure enough, a police vessel trailed them along the row of anchored ships. The captain lifted a radio to his mouth.

A loud curse reverberated from the bridge. The yacht engine roared and tipped as Aaron darted behind a barge. "We've got trouble in front of us, too."

Camille couldn't see any danger from the rear of the boat and hustled to the stateroom to look out the forward windows above the bed. Facing them head-on was a speedboat, as slick and tricked-out as the one they'd eluded three days earlier. Men with automatic rifles perched near the bow.

With her fist, Camille thumped the panel covering the secret cubby behind the headboard Aaron had punched out in case the police ever caught up to them and drew out an M16. She locked a magazine in place, loaded the chamber and shoved it into a pillowcase. No sense waving a high-powered automatic rifle at the police trailing them.

Covered rifle in hand, she ran full-speed to the back of the boat and up to the bridge. Aaron wrenched the yacht into another sharp U-turn, tipping it perilously to one side as he tried to put some space between them and the other boat.

But no sooner had they made a one-eighty turn than the police vessel appeared in front of them.

Behind them, a quick succession of shots fired out. The men aboard the police vessel drew their firearms and aimed in their direction.

"Damn it," Aaron barked. "We're caught in the cross fire."

Camille looked from the men with guns behind them to the police with guns before them. "What do you say we introduce our friends here to each other and get the hell out of the way?"

"You got it." He pushed the throttle to max velocity. Camille glanced behind them to see the speedboat hot on their tail. A hundred feet from the police vessel, Aaron wrenched the steering wheel in a sharp turn and threaded the yacht between two fishing boats.

Gunfire and shouting exploded behind them. Aaron dropped the yacht to an inconspicuous speed, aimed it in the direction of their new marina slip and let out a long, slow exhale.

Burdened by the crazy urge to throw her arms around him, she plunged her hands in her pockets and nudged Aaron's leg with her foot. "Nice work, Captain."

"Yeah, well, I wish I didn't have a reason to show off my boating skills." He offered her a weary half smile and raked his fingers through his hair. Funny, Camille wanted to do the same. Her gaze dropped to his mouth. The kiss they shared on the ridge above the desert compound seemed a lifetime ago.

Maybe he noticed her looking because he glanced her way and set his hand on her thigh. Her breath catching, she slipped from beneath his grasp before his warmth had the chance to penetrate her jeans. Her bum leg ached again after so much running around, so she leaned against the rail. "I identified a cartel member, back at the warehouses near the port."

"Seriously?"

"Yeah. I was coming to tell you when the police showed up."

"We need to check that out right away. Let's dock the boat and double back on the bike."

They sped along the waterfront by bike. After chaining it to a fence several blocks from the warehouse, they crept the rest of the way by foot, winding through the maze of buildings in the glow of the fading sun.

Camille's leg was killing her. Normally, she could walk for ten minutes before pain set in. To her mortification, her stride began to hitch with a limp. Aaron shot her a concerned look, but pressed on without a word until the black sedan became visible the next building over. He led the way into a truck bed, then atop the cab, hoisting himself another four feet onto the flat roof of the building. Camille glared at the hand he offered.

"Stubborn woman. Give me your hand."

"Get out of my way. If you can't treat me like an equal, this isn't going to work."

"Fine, Camille. You win this round. Why accept help when you can struggle to do something yourself." He kept up a string of grumbling as he moved away from the edge on his hands and knees.

Camille pulled herself up without a problem, like she knew she could. They crawled the length of the building until they had a perfect line of sight to the sedan, the men and the roll-up door behind them.

"The roll-up door's opening," Aaron whispered.

A run-down, boxy white delivery truck lumbered out.

Camille huffed in frustration. "Crap. We can't get back to the bike in time to follow it." She stared at its rear bumper, memorizing the license plate number.

"Look where it's headed," Aaron said.

Sure enough, the truck drove through the entrance gate of the ferry terminal, waved in by the passive guard. It coasted past the line of waiting vehicles and up the ramp into the bowels of the ferry.

The two guards still stood outside the now-empty garage. Two Down looked restless, glancing at his watch every minute or so as the ferry engine came to life. The ramp closed. Another few minutes passed, then the ferry engines grew louder as it backed slowly away from the port.

Aaron tipped his head in the ship's direction. "Where do you suppose it's headed?"

"Wait—I remember reading this." She squinted up toward the sky, sifting through her memory of the La Paz map she'd studied while laid up with her bum knee. "Across the Sea of Cortez, to Mazatlán."

Before the ferry had cleared the mouth of the bay, a man strolled out from the shadows of the open garage.

"Good God," Camille muttered. "Rodrigo Perez." Her breath froze in her lungs and her eyes refused to blink. She inched toward the roof's edge, praying for a sign of Rosalia—a little girl's tinkling laugh, a flash of pink fabric, a toy, anything. Aaron clamped a hand on her arm, in either support or warning, she couldn't tell.

Perez was a short man with a broad, muscled build. He impatiently flicked a cigarette between the fingers of his black leather glove as Two Down opened the sedan's door for him.

Aaron tipped his head toward Camille so his lips brushed her earlobe as he whispered, "I'm going to go out on a limb and guess this is the distribution part of the cartel's weapons-smuggling operation."

Tiny bumps raised on the skin of Camille's arms and the back of her neck at the contact. She shifted, putting some necessary space between them, then did a quick scan for security cameras, finding none. "This is a conspicuous location for illegal activity. If you're right and this is the distribution point for weapons or drugs, then they're relying on some pretty flimsy security."

Two Down closed the warehouse unit and locked it with a chain and padlock.

"We could have that padlock off without breaking a sweat using a bolt cutter," she added.

"Maybe there's an alarm system."

"Or nothing of value inside. Makes me wonder where Perez relocated all those crates of weapons to after abandoning the desert compound. I don't think this is the spot."

"Maybe this is only a pick-up point, not long-term storage," Aaron said.

Camille kept her eyes on Perez. "I bet you anything their new storage facility is wherever that black sedan's headed. And I bet Rosalia's there, too."

Two Down climbed behind the wheel of the car and put it in gear. Camille scrambled away from the edge and crawled back the way they'd come as fast as her arms and legs would go. "Let's move. We can't lose this lead. Not when we're so close."

The sedan rolled toward the warehouse's east exit. Aaron and Camille hustled along the building, peeking over the edge for the truck they'd made use of before, but the road was empty. Nothing except blacktop at the end of a twelve-foot drop.

Aaron snagged Camille's elbow and whirled her to face him. "This is how it's going to be and you're not going to argue with me. I'm going to drop first and catch you. Got it?"

"You don't need—"

"Zip it. I get to win this one."

Before she could protest further, he backed over the edge on his stomach and dropped. Camille repeated the shimmy over the side into a dangle.

"Okay," Aaron said, "one…two…three."

She let go, hating the feel of the free fall. Then her arms were around Aaron's neck and his hands were on her butt. He flashed a white-toothed smile and gave her a squeeze.

"Remember your no-groping promise." She cringed at the hint of hysteria in her tone.

Aaron scoffed and set her on her feet. "That wasn't a grope. That was a catch." He took off in a flat run to the bike, calling over his shoulder, "Besides, that promise expired."

Camille trotted after him, teeth clenched against the pain. "Promises don't expire."

He doubled back for her on the bike. She reached for the helmet, but he pulled it away.

"Camille, that promise expired."

She lunged for the helmet and jerked it away from him. They'd have to argue about it later because they finally had a lead to run down. She vaulted onto the back of the bike and it took off with a spine-rattling whine.

And just like that, the hunt was on.

Chapter 11

As far as drinking establishments went, the bar Camille and Aaron had stared at for three hours was as hospitable as a crematorium. There were windows, or rather, pieces of glass framed in the graffitied wall that weren't clean enough to see through. A small sign named the place Casa del Perro Negro—House of the Black Dog—words even Camille could translate. Next to the sign was a crudely painted silhouette of what Camille assumed was a black dog, but looked more like a goat, its stubby tail up and its mouth open.

The black sedan had entered a garage on the side of the two-story building that housed the bar and otherwise appeared vacant. The oddity of the building, with its uniformly closed curtains, dusty front stoop and lack of activity, sent up a red flag in Camille's mind. Something about this place was *wrong*.

Before settling at the taquería, they'd circled the block on the bike. A dead-end alley cut through one side of the building, guarded by a single, large Latino man neither Camille nor Aaron recognized. They continued around to the taquería, purchased warm bottles of cola and settled at a window table. Their main focus was on two equally huge men, probably bouncers, who perched on stools on either side of the bar's entrance.

As darkness settled over the city and the bouncers crossed their arms over their chests and hunkered down like birds preparing to sleep, Camille and Aaron grew restless. In their three-hour surveillance, not a single person had come or gone from the place.

"Perez and his crew have been inside for hours,"

Aaron said quietly. "That's a long time to sit in a bar."

"Makes me wonder if it's really a bar."

Aaron rubbed his chin. "Next time Perez and his men leave, I'd like to check it out."

"Me, too. I hate this. Rosalia could be in there, only a couple hundred feet away from us. I've got an idea, but we'll need to go shopping first. We can come back tomorrow, fully armed."

"Sounds like a date."

As they walked to the bike they'd chained in an alley several blocks away, Aaron draped his arm loosely around Camille's shoulders and kissed her temple. He was probably attempting to blend in with other couples they'd seen out for strolls, enjoying the crisp, clear evening. Even still, he ought not to confuse her heart that way, with casual tenderness that meant nothing to him.

When he kissed her a second time, she ground to a halt, twisting free of his arm. "Is this about what you said earlier? That your promises to me expired?"

"They have."

Camille's stomach tightened uncomfortably. It took her a good thirty seconds to wind her anger up. When it did, she grabbed his jacket by the collar and dragged him into the shadows of the nearest alley. Wagging a finger like a knife in front of his face, she let it rip.

"Allow me to send a message straight to your bloated ego, Aaron. You don't get to do whatever you want. When a woman says no, you back off. Rules don't expire because you think they should, you entitled jerk. I told you once and I'm telling you again now—no kissing, no groping. In fact, no touching at all."

He brushed her lips with his thumb. "You sure that's what you want?"

"Goddamn it," she shrieked, sweeping her leg across his to trip him. He let out a surprised howl and hit the ground on his knees.

Then her foot was on his back, pushing him to his stomach. She ground her knee into his ribs while twisting his right arm behind him at an awkward angle, pinning him.

"I hope I've got your attention, because it's the last time I'm going to say this. Stop. Touching. Me. From now on, you'll show me the respect I deserve. Got it?"

"You've made your point."

"Good."

"But I have a question. How will you be punishing me if I touch you again?"

"Damn it, Aaron, you're in no position to be condescending." She tugged on his twisted arm to illustrate her point.

"Okay, okay. Ouch."

She released him and stood. She hadn't meant to lose her cool and was sorry she'd hurt him, but he was hurting her more than he knew, his every touch and look a torturous reminder of what she could never have.

Aaron gingerly got to his feet, brushed gravel from his knees and shook out his arm. With an apologetic smile, he offered his hand to shake, which she accepted. Then he crushed her to the wall.

Camille gasped.

He held both her hands in one of his above her head and spanned his other hand along her collarbone. With his knees, he pried her legs apart and with his hips, he pinned her waist to the wall. Breathless with shock, Camille struggled to twist away from his grip, but he increased the pressure of his knees, hips and hands until she was helplessly immobile.

Helplessly aroused.

She shifted her hips to cradle his erection more comfortably and he reacted by pressing against her more adamantly. Squeezing her eyes shut, she rolled her head to the side, fighting a moan of pleasure as wet heat gathered between her thighs.

"It's your turn to listen now." He buried his nose in the hair behind her ear, making her toes curl. "Did it ever occur to you that I antagonize you on purpose, for the pleasure of seeing you all riled up? Hmm? Ever think of that?"

She couldn't look at him, much less speak, she was so angry with him for making her vulnerable, for exposing the depth of her attraction to him.

Well, *attraction* was a gross simplification. She wanted to taste every inch of his perfect body, to slip those flimsy boxers off his hips and discover exactly where the trail of hair under his navel led. She wanted Aaron so badly, she felt an emptiness that hurt worse than the memory of her accident, worse than her leg after running for hours from the Gigante Market.

He delicately brushed his closed lips over hers. It took all her strength not to open her mouth in offering.

"You see, when you're angry, you get a tiny crease between your eyebrows and the pulse on your neck is visible." He slid his fingers from her collarbone and found her pounding heartbeat at the base of her jaw.

"And when you're really, really angry like you are now, you flush the most fascinating shade of pink from your ears all the way to the skin between your breasts." He touched the tip of his tongue to her earlobe. When she shivered, he growled, "Every little bit of you is mine, Camille."

She kept her eyes closed, fighting hard to ignore the feel of his hands and mouth.

He pushed away from the wall. "You want me to quit riling you up? Stop looking so damned tempting every time you're mad."

He strode from the alley.

Camille sagged against the wall. Her body hummed with residual sensation, as though his tongue still lingered on her ear and the hard length of him still pressed against her. The urge to touch herself in the places that still tingled was overwhelming. She resisted, flattening her palms against the rough stucco behind her.

After a few more gulps of air, she pushed away from the wall and jogged to catch up with him, careful to keep a car's length of space between them until the moment she had no choice but to mount the bike behind him and secure her arms around his warm, hard body for the drive to the store for supplies for the morning's operation.

Camille was working way too hard, that was for sure. Ignoring someone on a thirty-three foot yacht with one bathroom and only a handful of places to sit was exhausting. She devoted all her energy for the rest of the night toward that end. When Aaron sat at the dining table, she relocated to the bridge. When he climbed to the bridge, smiling his million-watt dimpled smile, she returned to the cabin.

Infinitely relieved when he turned off the stateroom light and climbed into bed, Camille opted for the sofa. As she lay there, trying desperately to get comfortable on the narrow cushions, she had plenty of time to think. Aaron had, in essence, propositioned her, which she decided was the culmination of two things. One, she didn't fall all over him like the rest of the female population, which he undoubtedly considered a challenge. And two, this was probably the longest he'd gone without sex and Camille was the closest warm body. Sure, she let him hold her while they slept, but that was different. That was… Well, she wasn't sure why she'd let him get away with that, but she certainly wasn't going to let it happen again.

No matter the reason behind Aaron's behavior, Camille needed to be more diligent in her effort to keep her distance from him. It wasn't about holding a grudge or hoping for an apology, it was about preserving the last shreds of her heart from the man she'd wanted beyond reason from the moment she met him, the man who disliked her for two straight years until he was trapped with her in Mexico.

She couldn't stand the idea of becoming his temporary, forgettable relief—not even if it meant the end of her long-maligned and embarrassing virginity.

She'd saved her virginity like a jewel in high school. In college, when it no longer meant so much to her, she feared her inexperience would make her look the fool. Then the accident took away years of her life. Time and opportunities slipped by her until the potential embarrassment of revealing her inexperience trumped her curiosity and desire for sex. As if any men were waiting in line for the privilege.

Well, a man was waiting in line now.

But she cared too much about him to give herself freely, not when she meant nothing to him in return. Hugging herself, she stared at the night sky through the window above the sofa. *Rosalia, I'm going to find you. I swear. And then I'm going to get as far away from Aaron Montgomery as I can. Before my heart shatters any more than it already has.*

After two hours of tossing and turning and agonizing over things she could never have, Aaron appeared above her.

"I'm ignoring you."

"I noticed."

"Go away and let me sleep."

"You're not getting any more sleep than I am,

Camille." He worked his hands underneath her and lifted her into his arms. She considered fighting him but knew she'd only be fooling herself to deny that she'd let him do whatever he wanted.

"What are you doing?" she asked.

"Putting you back where you belong so we can get some rest."

"Oh." He only wanted to sleep. She was relieved…wasn't she?

He laid her on the bed and, instead of walking around to his side, had the audacity to climb over her—but only partially. His left leg and arm never made it over, but remained draped across her as if she was the world's first living, breathing full-body pillow.

"Mmm…that's better," he hummed softly, burrowing his face in her hair.

Camille stifled her own contented sigh.

Maybe she was approaching her needs all wrong. All her self-protection and fear of failure wasn't getting her very far in life. As she lay there in Aaron's embrace, on the precipice of sleep, she felt a shift in her perspective, as if the right sequence of numbers had finally been entered into the combination lock of a vault and it sat, ready to be opened. Perhaps it was time to set aside her fear. Perhaps it was time to change her life for the better.

Camille hated birthday celebrations. She hated the singling out, the special designation of a person not on the basis of merit, but simply because that person had survived another year. This distaste extended to other people's birthdays, but her own was the worst.

As a child, she begged her parents yearly to forgo her party. They compromised, agreeing to never mention her birthday to anyone outside the family so long as she accepted the fact that every February 20, she would endure cake and presents and singing and specialness, if only at their kitchen table.

It never occurred to her to tell Aaron today was her birthday. Not that she took turning thirty lightly. That she had survived to see this day was a milestone more significant than any other in her life. She just planned to mark the occasion privately.

As her gift, she had decided to reboot her mess of a life—assuming she made it out of Mexico alive. First off, she was going to quit her job. The police force had nothing left to offer her. She had enough money, both in savings and her portion of stolen cartel cash, that she could do anything she wanted, go anywhere she pleased.

She refused to live in fear anymore. If she survived Mexico, she wouldn't waste the rest of her life stubbornly clinging to her pride at the forfeit of her happiness. Aaron had been right, it was time she figured out how to be happy. No more laps in a pool, no more thankless job, no more lonely apartment. Maybe she'd take up scuba diving. Maybe she'd visit all seven continents. She definitely wanted to try skydiving again.

She rubbed the sleep from her eyes and sat up in bed. There was little point in dreaming of the future with a full day of cartel-hunting, child-rescuing danger ahead of her.

Today they were stealing inside the House of the Black Dog.

"Cam?" Aaron ducked his head through the stateroom door. "I'm docking the boat."

"I'll be ready."

Like the day she acted as police spokesperson for Rosalia's kidnapping, today she'd be costuming up again. She fished through the bag of items they bought the night before at Walmart. Grabbing the bikini, she headed to the bathroom.

An hour later, Camille and Aaron stood across the street from the bar at a bus stop, trying to look inconspicuous.

Aaron frowned. "Hmph. I don't think I like you wearing makeup. I mean, you're still beautiful, you always are, but it's not...you."

Camille, covered in a long coat, scowled as she balanced precariously in the cheaply made, strappy black heels that were digging into her feet.

Walmart was a great source for many things, but a mecca for shoes it was not.

"I'd rather you didn't critique my appearance." She winced at the hostility in her voice, but the shoes were making her grumpy.

Looking serenely at her, Aaron slid an arm around her waist and leaned closer.

"Camille." His whisper was as soft as a caress. "You are the most beautiful woman I've ever seen."

This wasn't how she wanted it to be between them. She didn't want him to lavish her with sweet words that were little lies. It hurt too much.

"Don't do that. Please." She squirmed in a half-hearted effort to break free of his grip, but she didn't want to draw attention from passersby.

"You don't want to hear it, I know. We haven't always gotten along, but..." His lips grazed her temple and nipped at her ear.

Camille's mouth went dry. She may have stopped breathing but it was hard to tell with the way her pulse started racing and her insides grew heavy, as if all her blood was relocating to the sensitive juncture of her thighs. What had she been about to say? She couldn't remember.

"I'm trying to be patient," Aaron murmured, "so I'm going to give you a little more time to think about what you want."

"What I want?" This was not going according to plan. She was supposed to be fending off his advances. While she was grateful that she retained the ability to speak, she couldn't get her brain past the urge to tear his clothes off.

"The clock's ticking, Camille."

"What?" Did she miss something? What clock?

"What I'm saying is, you've got a little more time to think about what you want before I haul you onto our bed and give you what I know you need."

Her knees wobbled. She was saved from having to form coherent thoughts by the opening of the garage door on the side of the building and the emergence of a familiar sedan.

Aaron released his hold on her waist. "Show-time."

Camille tried to snap her body out of its trance, but it had frozen.

"Camille? Let's go."

"Just a sec." She blinked, trying to clear the fuzz from her mind.

The sedan drove southeast, toward Pichilingue. As soon as it disappeared, Aaron patiently removed her hand from his shirt collar, one finger at a time.

Aaron watched Camille walk south in order to approach the alley from the opposite direction. Once she was out of view, he walked the dirt bike around the north side and propped it against the wall a few feet from the alley entrance.

He gripped his gun, concealing it inside his jacket. Then he waited anxiously for Camille to reappear. She'd call him a chauvinistic jackass again for entertaining such a thought, but he hated to have her out of his sight for even a minute.

As his anxiety mounted, she rounded the corner, walking toward him. The entrance of the alley gaped between them like a chasm. Setting her voluminous orange beach bag on the ground, she removed her coat.

Aaron's mouth went dry. He'd seen the red swimsuit she purchased, but he hadn't thought much about how it would actually look painted on her creamy-skinned, curvaceous body. Oblivious to his dismay, she gave him a determined nod and stumbled purposefully, spilling the contents of the bag. Hair spray, lipsticks and other womanly goodies rolled, exactly as planned, into the alley. Camille chased after the scattering contents, bridging the distance to the guard.

Sure enough, as soon as he caught sight of her, the man rose from his stool and sauntered her way, lecherously appraising her body. Thank God Camille didn't understand Spanish. Aaron, on the other hand, understood every single filthy word. While her bikini had been an unwelcome surprise, he was even less prepared for the rage that surged through him as he listened to the guard demean her.

The plan was for Aaron to hold his shot until the guard was standing near the Dumpsters in the middle of the alley. Aaron stood with his finger on the trigger of his gun and tried to be patient. But when the guard unzipped his pants and told Camille to get on her knees like the whore she was, Aaron pivoted into view and put two bullets through his chest.

Camille looked questioningly at Aaron but said nothing. They dragged the body between the Dumpsters, out of view from the street. While Aaron repositioned the bike in the alley for a getaway vehicle, Camille changed into sneakers, a T-shirt and shorts from her bag. She dropped the heels in the Dumpster, slung her rifle over her shoulder and got out a handgun with silencer—going from eye candy to warrior in seconds flat.

With Camille in the lead, they skulked into the bar.

Chapter 12

The bar was empty.

No people, no tables or chairs, no alcohol. Exchanging a worried look with Camille, Aaron checked the solitary bathroom—empty. They took positions against the wall next to the front door. He pushed it open a few inches to get the bouncers' attention and stepped back into the shadows, hoping the men were curious sorts.

They were.

The bouncers advanced into the room with their guns drawn. Aaron aimed, as did Camille, only her gun hand shook so badly he couldn't see how she'd hit her target. Damn. He forgot about that complication. Without waiting to see if she got control of her aim, he shot both guards in the back. Camille fired, but her bullet lodged in the wall behind the bar.

She closed her eyes. When she reopened them, she nodded to Aaron with a look of cool determination. He squeezed her shoulder in a show of encouragement and motioned to the interior door on the far side of the room.

He tested the knob. Unlocked. Widening his stance, he put his finger on the trigger of his gun and gestured for Camille to open the door.

It only took a second to realize what a mistake they'd made.

At least a half dozen sets of eyes fixed on them from inside the room, which had been made up to look like a living room with sofas and a television. A little girl was seated on the floor.

At the first crack of gunfire from the room, Camille cursed and took off in a dead run for the alley, with Aaron outpacing her through the bar and onto the bike. Their helmets lay abandoned in the alley as they peeled away.

In no time, two Jeeps pulled into view, tailing Aaron and Camille and gaining ground fast. Aaron gunned it, but the Jeeps kept up with the punishing pace.

They flew through the city, negotiating the cars and people, ignoring stoplights and signs. Aaron shot west through the outlying neighborhoods of town where the roads were wider and less crowded. He took every possible shortcut through dirt lots and alleys but could not lose the Jeeps.

They sped past the airport, then the highway that marked the last vestiges of civilization, into the open desert. The landscape of Baja was denser than the California desert, but Aaron was banking on his experience with all-terrain vehicles as a Park Ranger to gain the advantage.

The butt of Camille's rifle poked him in the ribs. Aaron tried to keep the bike steady while she sprayed a quick staccato of shots. A loud screech and clattering sounded behind them.

"What's happening?" he yelled.

"One Jeep down, one to go."

The men in the remaining Jeep fired back. It sounded as though they only had handguns, but a bullet was a bullet.

Camille and Aaron's best hope of survival was to stay unpredictable. With that in mind, Aaron took each foothill fast, jumping dried riverbeds and weaving around the shrubs and rocks while Camille continued to fire.

"How many men?" he asked.

"Three—the driver and two shooters." They were fired at twice and Camille responded with another cluster of shots. "Check that, one shooter now."

Aaron swerved around a boulder the size of a shack and realized too late they were approaching a huge fissure in the earth too wide to jump and too near to stop or turn. Putting on the brakes, he pushed Camille off the bike and attempted a controlled crash. The momentum was too great. He and the downed bike skidded into the fissure.

Camille crawled to the edge. "Aaron!"

He clung to a tiny outcropping on the inner wall, his shoes pedaling against the side.

The rumble of an engine warned them of the Jeep's approach.

"Stay there," she whispered, scrambling out of view. Her rifle discharged a dozen more rounds. Aaron prayed she was hidden behind a boulder as the men's return fire echoed through the fissure.

The Jeep's engine cut out and a man shouted in English at Camille to freeze. A shuffle of feet on the sandy ground made Aaron brace for discovery, but no one peeked over the edge. Maybe they didn't realize he was there.

A sharp smack of flesh hitting flesh reverberated in the quiet, and Camille grunted softly.

They were hitting her. The men were hitting his Camille.

Aaron dug deep, finding a strength he didn't know he had. He pulled up on the ledge and got a toe on it, then a knee. He pocketed a handful of sand, then got out his gun.

Smack. A man's laughter.

"Is that all you got?" Camille sneered in a hoarse voice.

In a state of focused fury, Aaron surrendered to the most ancient, savage part of his being. He vaulted out of the fissure with gun drawn.

Only one man was hurting Camille. A body lay slumped over the Jeep's passenger door as blood pooled on the dirt below.

Aaron took aim at the short, mustachioed, middle-aged Mexican who had Camille by the hair, jamming her own rifle into her shoulder as she knelt on the ground. The man's eyes were wide, as if Aaron had surprised him. Good.

"Aaron, you idiot. You should have saved yourself. Now we'll both die."

Aaron ignored her. He sized up her captor and plotted his next move.

"Drop your gun or I kill her," the man shouted in heavily accented English. He sounded nervous, as if he was in way over his head. Aaron knew exactly how to play this guy. He took a few steps forward.

"Forget about me. Kill him."

Unable to resist the impulse, he snorted. "You're killin' me with your whole martyr thing, Cam." He put his hand in his pocket as casually as possible, gathering sand.

"Drop the gun…now," the man hollered.

Aaron raised his arms in surrender, then took a few more steps forward and placed his gun on the ground too near to Camille for her captor to let it stay there. When the man let go of her hair and reached for the gun, Aaron flung the sand into his eyes, blinding him. Grabbing the rifle's nose, he deflected it into the sand as it fired.

The man doubled over with his hands covering his face, shrieking in pain. Aaron gripped the handle of the spare gun he'd stashed in a makeshift holder between his shoulder blades. He killed the bastard with a single shot, right through his ear.

Camille, under the light of the full moon, glowed an ethereal shade of blue. She sat in the cocaptain's chair, clad in loose-fitting white pants and a white T-shirt, hugging herself and gazing at the distant sea, exactly as Aaron left her when he went to wash the sand and blood spatter from his hair and skin.

After driving the cartel's Jeep to the outskirts of town, they'd snagged a taxi ride to the marina. The whole time, Aaron's nerves were a jumble of live wires. He never took his hand off the gun hidden beneath his shirt, nor his eyes off their surroundings, anticipating ambush at every turn. Even on the boat, after he'd anchored in the cove of an uninhabited island two hours from the mouth of the bay, he still didn't feel safe.

He wasn't sure if he'd ever feel safe again.

They'd survived the day but in infiltrating the cartel's hideout and killing more of its operatives, the targets on their backs were bigger than ever.

When Aaron cleared his throat to alert Camille of his presence, she looked at him and shivered. He removed the black flannel shirt he'd donned over his T-shirt and held it out in offering. She shook her head.

"Don't argue with me. Not tonight."

After a moment's hesitation, she accepted the shirt. He helped her on with it, then settled in the captain's chair. The sight of Camille wearing his clothes was unexpectedly erotic. The collar pressed against her cheeks, accentuating the ivory glow of her skin and her slender fingers peeking out from the cuffs. Their eyes met and she shivered again.

Aaron felt the air surrounding them charge, crackling with electric current. He swallowed, then gestured to her bare feet. "I'll bring you some socks."

Mechanically, he walked through the cabin and found a pair of her socks. Camille watched his approach with eyes as black as the flannel shirt, as deep as the night around her. He sat and swiveled her chair to face his.

With a racing pulse, he brought her feet to his lap and inched his fingers up the lengths of her calves inside her pants. He'd never touched her here, not like this.

"Aaron, stop." Her voice was breathy, aroused. He stopped but didn't release his hold on her leg. "I don't…I don't want…"

"Don't try to tell me you don't want me, Camille. I know you better than that."

He captured her right foot in his hands. It was velvet against his calloused palms.

"You don't know me at all."

What a load of crap she was feeding herself. He'd spent every moment of the past week memorizing her—from her body to the cadence of her speech, every sigh and every look. He'd lain awake each night listening to her breathe, drenching his senses with the feel and scent of her hair, her skin. He knew Camille Fisher as well as he knew himself, better perhaps. "What have you convinced yourself of? What's going on in that sharp mind of yours?"

"I…"

As she searched for words, he cradled her foot, warming it.

"I don't want this between us."

He tipped her chin up until she looked into his eyes. "Baby, it's already between us."

The torment in her expression spoke of a battle raging within her. She knew he was right.

"If you tell me to stop again, I will. But you know as well as I do there's no changing the truth. Even if we never act on the way we feel, this will always be here between us."

She stiffened and, for a moment, Aaron thought he'd ruined his chance. His fingers froze on her foot. He sucked in a frustrated breath.

Her right hand twisted the flannel as she seemed to consider his words.

She met his gaze, her green eyes piercing, as if testing his merit, weighing his honor. *Trust me, Camille. Let me show you how we could be together.*

With a nod, she slipped low in the chair and her knees fell open. It was sexy as hell.

Releasing the breath he'd been holding, he slid both thumbs along the arch. Her breath stuttered. Suppressing a smile, he concentrated on her foot, kneading and exploring, rolling each toe and sliding his index finger between them. She squirmed and purred softly, a response that ignited within Aaron something wholly atavistic. Before this night was over, every secret little place on her, previously ignored, was going to be branded by him.

He brought her leg to his mouth and kissed the inside of her ankle, tasting it with his tongue. She slouched further in the chair and her legs gaped apart. Aaron froze, not trusting himself to move one millimeter until he overcame the urge to take her right then and there.

Once he regained mastery over himself, he scooted forward and guided her feet up the lengths of his thighs until her toes touched the crease of his hips. He lifted his eyes to gauge her demeanor again. A corner of her lips turned up in a lazy smile. It was all he needed to see.

He pulled her onto his lap so she was straddling him.

Their bodies and mouths united like water hitting hot oil, the power of two opposing forces colliding. They kissed violently, openmouthed, tongues pushing and testing, nostrils flared with the strain of breathing, each taking and consuming the other. Demanding more. Camille's hands were in Aaron's hair and around his neck, clinging to him.

This time, he couldn't stop his mouth from curling into a hard smile, or his eyes from reflecting the possessiveness radiating through him. He tugged on the collar of her shirt, exposing her shoulder, and feasted on her sweet skin, only half aware of her own exploration of him. Her mouth sucked at his neck and earlobe. Her fingers remained threaded through his hair except for every so often, when she framed his face with her hands and forced his mouth back to hers.

The ferocity of her passion was what he'd been waiting for night after torturous night. He wanted her to hunger the way he hungered. To need like he needed. He licked a trail from her collarbone to the skin between her breasts. She moaned and tipped her chin up, arching to him.

It had been worth the wait.

When he was ready to do away with her clothes, he lifted her off him, back into her own chair. Crossing her arms, she gazed at the horizon in a show of prideful restraint—as though she thought he was done with her. The crease between her eyebrows appeared and, even in the shadows, the hard clench of her jaw was apparent.

So strong, yet so fragile, she would never beg him for more. If he walked away at that moment, she'd never breathe a word about their kiss, never let the shield guarding her vulnerability crack. What happened to her that made her demand so little of others, so much of herself? It was a question for another time. Tonight, he had far more important discoveries to make.

He stroked her cheek and turned her face up to his.

"I'm going to take you to our bed and make love to you now."

* * *

It was harder than Camille expected to give herself over to passion from a safe emotional distance.

She'd sat on the bridge, replaying Aaron's words outside the bar that morning in her head, confused and aroused. Terrified. As far as birthday resolutions went, hers was off to a dismal start. As a gift to herself, she'd vowed to let go of the stilted, fearful woman she'd become. To experience life to the fullest. To discover happiness. And yet, she'd lingered on the bridge that night, too scared to face Aaron within the confines of the cabin, praying he'd leave her alone so she could ignore the desire that was eating her from the inside out.

Pathetic.

And then he was on the bridge, looming over her, his eyes dark with desire. She didn't want to accept his flannel shirt, knowing it would smell of him—and it had. Rich and masculine, clean. *Aaron.* The fabric was damp and hinted at the shampoo he'd used. She'd turned up the collar and inhaled.

His skilled hands had touched her in a way no man had before, but it was his words that tipped her over the edge.

There's no changing the truth. This will always be here between us.

He was right. No matter how desperately she fought against her feelings for him, they would never change. Never burn out. Never leave her at peace. She had only one way to combat the fear that held her back—to bulldoze straight through it. To strike it down as it had stricken her for too many years.

So what if her desire for Aaron terrified her? So what if she was one more in a long line of conquests? He'd made her an offer and she'd be a hypocrite not to take him up on it.

The minute their clothes came off, her lack of experience would be obvious. She only hoped she wouldn't have to admit how inexperienced she actually was. But if he figured it out, if her hymen was miraculously still intact…there might be no getting around the truth. But she was no longer willing to let fear and pride hold her back.

Happy birthday, girl.

Aaron wasn't making it easy on her, though. She'd banked on his goofy sense of humor to emerge, for him to infuse the experience with playful banter and teasing smiles, but tonight he was dead serious. Did he dive into all his conquests' skins as if he was having them for dinner?

Did he always call it *making love?*

To counter her rising anxiety, she resolved to do the opposite of her fearful instincts for the rest of the night. So after her shirt was dispatched to the cabin floor by Aaron with lightning-quick efficiency and her instincts demanded she call the whole thing off, she grabbed fistfuls of his shirt and ripped it over his head. Then she did what she'd longed to for two long years. She caressed every single muscle of his rippling abs.

They shuffled past the sofa while kissing. Aaron

reached around her and punched on a light in the kitchenette.

"Turn around and put your hands on the table."

It was a command spoken softly, but a command nonetheless.

Despite the screaming protests of her instincts, she faced the table and set her palms on it, surprised at the pulse of pleasure it gave her to give up control to him. If she were keeping score, pleasure would be leading instinct two to nothing.

With his thumbs hooked in her waistband, Aaron shoved her pants to the ground. Pinning her to the table with his lower body, he dived into the skin of her neck, which was about the most delicious feeling Camille had ever experienced. She arched into his touch and when his teeth bit gently into the skin of her shoulder, she whimpered helplessly.

He unsnapped her bra and threw it on the table.

She twisted around, but he pushed her shoulder back and gently, but firmly, took her wrist and replaced her hands on the table, adding a squeeze of admonition.

He knelt and ran a finger along the side hem of her panties, beneath her buttocks and around to the front, until only thin, damp fabric separated his finger from where she really wanted it. His tongue followed his finger. Hunching into her arms, Camille put her head down, dizzy with sensation.

His teeth nipped at her inner thigh. His nose brushed against the panties. She widened her stance, wanting desperately for him to bury his finger or tongue in her. But instead of lingering, his lips skimmed across her panties and he continued the trek around her other thigh.

Finally, he slid her panties down and stood. Setting his hands over hers, he lifted their entwined fingers and straightened so that they were looking at their reflection in the window. She didn't recognize the woman she saw, half-naked and flushed with passion. Her breasts hung in the forefront, her nipples hardened with arousal. He moved their hands as one to cup her breasts, so that, really, she was the one doing the holding and he was the puppet-master. They felt foreign in her hands, plump and sensual.

She looked past her reflection to Aaron and gasped in shock. His eyes were fierce, and the muscles of his arms twitched like they did when he was agitated. That threw her off. He was enjoying it, too, wasn't he? Where was the Aaron she knew, the one with the dimples and the joyous laugh? Was she doing something wrong?

"Aaron…"

"Hmm?"

"I… Are you—"

Words failed her as he moved their joined right hands between her thighs. He manipulated his hold so both their index fingers swirled over the swollen pearl of nerve endings made slick with honeyed wetness. She writhed, straining to increase the pressure on this most sensitive part of her. He worked their fingers expertly until the world around Camille disappeared. All that existed was her raw need and the tips of their fingers.

Release swept like a strike of lightning through her body. She threw her head against his shoulder with a cry, the ferocity of her climax rocking them both where they stood locked together.

"You're mine," he rumbled into her ear.

The intensity of his tone made her eyes snap open. She studied his reflection and saw his first smile of the night—a savage grin that left her wondering how dimples could look so wicked.

Overcome with self-awareness, her urge to put some distance between them was a powerful one. But her instincts hadn't done her a lick of good, so now was hardly the time to let fear take over. Scared as hell but too stubborn to quit, she sunk to her knees and unfastened his jeans. It was time to even the playing field.

The jeans were the easy part—button off, zipper down and a tug. It was the boxers underneath that gave her pause. She had no idea what to do with Aaron's erection. Or rather, she had a general idea, but not many specific details and zero experience. She braced herself for the big reveal of her naïveté, then dropped the boxers to the floor and drew a sharp breath.

She'd seen a few male appendages in her day, but she'd never seen anything like this. All the jokes she'd made over the years about his tricked-out sports car compensating for something now seemed ridiculously inappropriate.

Aaron was huge. Monster.

She hesitantly grazed the shaft with her finger and watched it bob in response. Emboldened, she moved to the tip, slid the foreskin back and closed her mouth over the head. His body dipped and he staggered back, slamming into the kitchen counter. The muscles of her core pulsed with impatience, even as she grinned at the discovery that she had the power to do that to him. Oh, this could easily become her obsession, this piece of Aaron's anatomy.

Happy birthday, girl. Here's a bonus gift....

Before her exploration had barely begun, he

pushed her away. "You're going to have to tor-ment me on your own time." His voice was husky. "I've got other plans for you tonight."

He led her down the stairs. The light from the kitchenette filtered onto the bed like a spotlight into which she was tossed with alarming ease. Crawling up the length of her body, he kicked her legs apart with his knees. Then, beginning with her breasts, he proceeded to drive her into a frenzy with his tongue.

Moments before her second orgasm shattered her last threads of control, two random thoughts floated across her mind. The first was that if prac-tice made perfect then maybe she should thank Aaron for being such a male slut. And the sec-ond was that she was an idiot for waiting so long to have sex.

With an echoing scream, she clamped her thighs around his head. He kept his tongue on her, rid-ing her waves of pleasure until they subsided, then kissed his way back up her body. Breathing hard, he positioned himself on his knees between her legs. She thought briefly about using protection but dismissed the idea. They were fifty miles from shore, fighting for their lives in a foreign country. They couldn't simply dash to a store for supplies. The universe would just have to forgive her this one indiscretion on her birthday, because short of the fires of hell rising up around them, she wouldn't have stopped Aaron for anything.

He positioned himself at her entrance, then swirled his fingertips through her moisture. With his thumb caressing her tender flesh, he dipped his fingers inside her.

"You're so tight."

That was the understatement of the century.

His massive girth was bound to make this part a bit of a challenge. She tried to relax, determined to lose her virginity to Aaron no matter how long it took her body to accommodate him.

She wrapped her legs around his waist. "Is that a problem?" she teased.

The shadow of a smile crossed his face. He pressed forward gently, and she felt him hit a wall. Two sets of eyes flew open.

Chapter 13

"Is that…? Are you…?"

"Yes, I think it is. I'm a virgin." She screwed up her mouth in a wince. "Damn it. I have the worst luck in the world."

Thoughts swirled so furiously in Aaron's head that his brain seemed near the verge of exploding. He made to rock back on his heels, but the grip of Camille's legs around his hips proved unyielding. How could a woman as beautiful as Camille, surrounded by men on the job every day as she was, not once give herself over to passion? Or not even passion, but a down and dirty screw? Leave it to

Little Miss Martyr to deny herself such a fundamental human need.

Still reeling, he met her brilliant green eyes and recognized a familiar determination in them.

"But I turned thirty today, so don't you think it's time I did something about it?"

That knocked the wind from his sails. And here he thought they were making progress on the intimacy front. "Today's your birthday? Weren't you going to tell me?"

"I didn't see a reason to."

Ah, baby. What a way to live, inside herself, alone.

But no more.

She wouldn't be lonely again. Because she had him, and he knew on an elemental level that he would never let her go. He had no idea where the knowledge came from, or what it meant for their future, but it burned inside him as fiercely as his desire. And, oh, did he burn with desire for her. He looked down, drinking in her juicy curves, amazing breasts and full lips. Her tight, wet body ready to be claimed by him. She was a virgin. She was his to take.

Battling that caveman part of him urging him forward, he kissed her temple. His hands trembled and his muscles strained, holding back his body's demand. "Are you sure this is what you want?"

Cupping his cheeks, she searched his face. "More than anything."

At her answer, a feeling like a howl swept through him and he let go of his restraint. Thrusting deeply, he took her virginity.

She nuzzled her face against his shoulder. He held motionless but for the heavy rise and fall of his lungs. The significance of the moment crushed the last vestiges of the restless, spoiled boy he'd been before the kidnapping that changed everything, before he fell in love with Camille. "A part of you belongs to me now," he rasped, aware of his possessive tone but unable to prevent it.

"I know," she whispered softly, stroking his dampened hair away from his temple.

He took her mouth in a kiss laced with only the

slightest suggestion of tenderness. Then he began to move, determined to coax Camille's body toward ecstasy for the third time that night.

The longer Camille lay in Aaron's arms, listening to his even breathing, the worse she felt. She should have known better than to give her body to a man she cared about, not when it was just another roll in the hay for him. What a mess she'd created.

It turned out her greatest naïveté wasn't that of sexual inexperience, but of the way she'd believed she could separate her physical needs from her emotional ones. On the verge of a panic attack, she slid out of the room and found her clothes on the dark cabin floor.

The kitchen light turned on.

"Come back to bed," Aaron said quietly.

Camille glanced up and then away. She couldn't look at his perfect, nude body—such a painful reminder of how far out of her league he was. "Look, you don't need to pretend, not with me."

"What do you mean?"

"I'm not stupid. I knew I'd be another notch on your bedpost and I thought that would be okay. I didn't expect to feel so cheap afterward." She swallowed a lump in her throat.

Aaron tugged on her wrist, dragging her against him. "I won't let you belittle what happened here tonight. Look at me, Camille."

She could not. Never in her life had she felt so weak. And over what—a man?

He waited silently until she decided to get the inevitable battle over with and met his eyes.

"You don't think you mean anything to me, is that it?"

"Yeah, that's it."

He huffed. "Every single time I've had to make a choice, I've chosen you. Think about that. I've been with you every step you've taken and I've given you everything I have to give—my trust, my support, whatever is left of my life."

"That's your pride talking, Aaron. You can't stand that I'm not falling all over myself with grat-

itude for the privilege of being bedded by you."
A noise akin to thunder rolled through him. Camille felt the vibrations through her fists. Her resolve wavered, but it was too late to turn back.
She'd dug her own grave and it was time to get
in it. "Don't get me wrong, I'm relieved to be rid
of my virginity, but that's all tonight was about.
Nothing more."

Aaron's eyes were hard as stone. "Let me get
this straight. You were using me?"

"Right." Oh, the lies she told.

"You don't need anyone, is that it?"

"I don't need anyone, especially you."

He pressed his forehead against her temple, his
lips close to her ear. "Liar."

The word rippled through her like a puff of acrid
smoke. She pushed against him. "Let me go." She
had to get out of the situation before she broke
down and begged him to forgive her.

His grip on her intensified before he abruptly
released her. She stumbled back.

Aaron's features had taken on a sheen of anger,

his eyes narrow, his muscles rigid. "I'm not going to beg you to be with me." His voice was tight with control. "But this conversation is far from over. Consider yourself warned."

He walked into the stateroom and shut the door.

Camille let out the breath she'd been holding and closed her eyes. Like everything else in her life, her thirtieth birthday had gone horribly wrong. Sure, she was no longer a virgin, but the price to her heart had been too steep.

According to the *Los Angeles Times,* Camille and Aaron were dead.

Three days after Camille's birthday, Aaron read the headline at a marina newsstand after picking up a package from Dreyer at a shipping store. Doing his best to play it cool, he piled a stack of local and international newspapers into his arms and handed a large bill to the cashier before hurrying back on board.

They'd laid low in the waters north of La Paz without daring to venture near the city until they'd formulated a new plan. It had taken them a day of brainstorming, but they had one now and it was worth breaking their own rule of trusting no one to contact Dreyer. Aaron didn't actually think Dreyer was the one who'd ratted their location out to the cartel, but since they'd cut off communications with the outside world, the ambushes had stopped. There was no arguing with results like that. Still, their plan required technological equipment neither of them were savvy enough to create from scratch.

Dreyer supported their idea, which was why a small cardboard box now sat on the kitchen counter. But before dealing with that, Aaron was itching to read what the newspapers had to say about him.

At the dining table, he pored over the papers. On the front page of the *L.A. Times,* a color photo of Rosalia's mother clutching a picture of her daughter at a candlelight vigil accompanied an article on the stalled negotiations between the Mexican and American governments on the girl's recovery.

Aaron's heart clenched at the sobering reminder of what he and Camille were fighting for.

He turned the page and blinked back, caught off guard by a black-and-white still picture from a grainy video of a crowd of masked, armed men watching two bodies burn on a pyre. "Hey, Camille, according to the *Times,* the Cortez Cartel released a video of our deaths."

"Is that so?" She angled for a better view. "Looks like the paper's convinced the bodies are us. That's pretty shoddy journalism."

"The journalist tacks on a disclaimer that no indisputable proof of the bodies' identities has emerged, but—the journalist asks—why would the cartel lie about the murder of two Americans instead of continuing to use their captives as leverage?"

"I'm guessing it's because they don't want to show weakness by admitting their prisoners escaped."

Aaron skimmed a Mexican paper. "Get this—according to this paper, the only logical explanation for escalating violence in La Paz is that a rival cartel has moved in. Only no cartel—including the powerful La Mérida Cartel—had claimed responsibility for the violence. So the papers are making the leap of logic that an unknown cartel had entered the fray. The Ghost Cartel."

Camille broke out in laughter so genuine that Aaron stopped reading to watch the way her face lit up. God, she was beautiful. "I can't believe we've earned a nickname. That's terrible."

Aaron forced his gaze back to the paper before she had a chance to notice him gawking. "Listen to this. Mexican authorities' latest grisly discovery of three bodies in a Dumpster behind what appeared to be an abandoned hideout disguised as a bar brings the body count of dead Cortez operatives to nine in fourteen days. The city of La Paz is on the verge of a lockdown, with the mayor threatening curfews and stoppages of airline flights should the bloodshed continue."

"You need to call Dreyer, make sure our families know we're alive and well."

"When we spoke yesterday, he assured me our families have been warned that ICE is going to keep our escape on the down low. Hopefully they don't believe everything they read."

With an incredulous shake of his head, Aaron set the newspapers aside. Reading about his own death was bizarre, but not the only extraordinary thing to happen to Aaron while in Mexico. He didn't believe in fate and he definitely didn't believe in luck, but he'd always believed in his ability to create success by keeping his eyes open for unexpected opportunities. It was a fine theory and had led to many wonderful experiences in his life…right up until he realized that for two full years, he'd been blind to the fact that the woman he'd convinced himself to hate was actually his soul mate.

The tricky part was waiting for her to admit they belonged together. He could tell that on some level she'd figured it out…and was scared witless about it.

He wasn't sure how to alleviate her fears, wasn't

even sure what she was afraid of and couldn't decide how to start a conversation about it. Would professing his love help the situation or scare her more? Until he figured it out, he'd decided to give her a lot of space, which was pretty much torture given how small the yacht was. He didn't touch her, tried not to watch her and didn't hassle her about her choice to spend nights on the sofa, though he suffered from absolute sleeplessness and knew she did the same.

Feigning indifference to her bordered on intolerable, so instead Aaron gave all his energy over to rescuing Rosalia Perez and digging up enough intel on the Cortez Cartel to shut down the cartel's weapons-smuggling operation and put Rodrigo Perez behind bars for life.

With that goal in mind, he opened the package from Dreyer and poured a state-of-the-art tracking device and GPS locator onto the table. "Looks good. Now we have to figure out how to get close enough to the cartel delivery truck to put this on."

Camille lifted the device, studying it. "The next

ferry departure will be Tuesday. If the delivery truck's on it, it'll be locked up for the eighteen-hour trip. That's our window. That's when we plant the device."

"I like the way you think."

"Only problem is getting on board the ferry without ID."

"Very few people are above accepting a bribe if it's big enough. Hopefully that includes the ferry staff. I'm willing to risk it if you are."

"I am, absolutely."

"We can hire a private charter to Mazatlán. I've seen plenty of them around. Then we only need to bribe our way onto the ferry for the return trip."

Camille powered up the GPS locator. "I used a device like this on the job once upon a time. Unlike this model, that one had a self-destruct feature. Jacob and I used the explosion as a diversion while we breached a security fence. I might not have been able to build a tracking device, but I could definitely manage a bomb. What do you think?"

"Have you ever built a bomb?" Aaron asked.

"No, but I took a seminar on bomb defusing during Special Forces training, so I have a basic knowledge. I say we buy a cheap laptop and tap into an unsecured Wi-Fi signal, let the internet teach us the rest. I can handle—"

He glanced up to see Camille's gaze fixed on the window. He followed her line of sight to their reflection and straightened. The air surrounding them crackled with the tension of too many things left unsaid.

The last time they stood before this table, he'd brought her to orgasm with his finger. He'd watched her glorious, supple body writhe and shudder with pleasure in his arms. She'd whispered his name when she came. Every time she came that night. Under her breath, like a prayer or a curse. He wondered if she was conscious of doing that, wondered if she'd say his name again right now if he lifted her to the table and sunk his tongue into her sweet flesh.

Closing his eyes, he swallowed hard as the searing need to possess her ignited within him. He harnessed it, but barely, and opened them again to find her watching him through the reflection, her expression anxious and her skin flushed pink.

"I see you, Camille."

She stopped breathing. Her eyes grew wider.

"You're trying to hide from me, but you can't. I see you."

Her fingers shot out to tinker nervously with the tracking device. He settled his hand over hers and she stilled.

It was her turn to close her eyes. She shifted her body weight to lean against him as her head tilted back to rest on his shoulder, exposing the slender length of her neck. He grazed her skin with closed lips, wanting to stake his claim on her body with his teeth. Holding himself in check.

She sucked in a ragged breath and tensed. Twisting her hand from under his, she broke free of his hold, walked from the table and picked up her bike helmet. "Let's get out of here." Her voice was hoarse and trembling. "We have a bomb to build and we're wasting time."

It took several hours of research and shopping to come up with a blueprint and materials, but it was disturbingly easy how two people—foreigners, at that—could make up their minds to build a bomb and, within the same day, gather everything they needed.

Because their dirt bike was lying in a ravine in the desert, they took a taxi to a used motorbike lot and bought a new one. They then bought a cheap laptop and tapped into an internet signal at a downtown coffeehouse. Without much searching, they found easy-to-follow instructions for creating an explosive with a remote detonator. Walmart and two different hardware stores supplied almost everything else, except dynamite.

For that, they waited until midnight to cruise by the numerous construction sites that dotted the landscape between La Paz and Pichilingue. At a partially erected resort being carved into a cliff along the bay, they found what they were looking for behind a short chain-link fence, next to a portable office trailer. Camille's flashlight zeroed in on a nondescript metal supply shed secured by a chain and padlock.

With newly purchased bolt cutters, Aaron clipped a hole in the fence and they slipped in. The debris-strewn construction zone showed no signs of life, no security teams or guard dogs, only silent excavators and bulldozers that lay like sleeping giants amid innumerable pallets of pavers and Dumpsters.

The supply shed was a cinch to open with the cutters. The crate of dynamite was clearly marked with bright red lettering. *¡Cuidad! ¡Explosivos!* Aaron carefully plucked five sticks from the shredded-paper packing filler and nestled them into a backpack.

They were back on board the *Happily Ever After* before the moon hit the mountain ridges to the west of the city. After anchoring the boat on the leeward coast of a tiny island, Aaron joined Camille at the kitchen table, poring over the directions and sorting through their purchases.

"This is going to take some time. I don't want to make a mistake and blow us up."

"Gotta say, I'm happy to hear that. Anyhow, you have two days until Tuesday's ferry departure. If you need even more time, the delivery truck usually skips Thursday's ferry and goes out again on Saturday. Do what you have to do to get it right because if we screw up this chance, Perez and his men will go so deep underground, we might never find Rosalia."

Saturday afternoon, six days after Camille began building the bomb, both the *Puerto Azul* and the suddenly cash-flush cocaptains of *Sea Dreamin',* a private yacht charter, embarked on the eighteen-hour journey across the Sea of Cortez, the former transporting an unmarked delivery truck most likely filled with weapons and the latter transporting a pair of American newlyweds to the next destination of their honeymoon...or so Aaron and Camille's story went.

The bomb had been ready for the Tuesday ferry, but the cartel delivery truck had been nowhere in sight. Terrified that this, their only lead, had dried up, on Saturday they waited on the bike near the ferry terminal with frayed nerves until they caught a first glimpse of the delivery truck. They watched it drive up the ferry ramp on Saturday at noon, then took off toward the cluster of yacht charters vying for tourist dollars near the public marina.

Once at sea, Camille and Aaron settled onto a bench on the back deck of the *Sea Dreamin'*. As the sun set over the Baja peninsula and the water faded from cerulean to onyx as the sky darkened, the air turned cool and crisp. Camille tensed her muscles against a shiver, then glanced at Aaron to gauge if he'd noticed, but he was staring at her hand clutching the seat cushion. With a twitch of movement, he reached for it.

Inhaling sharply, she leaped to her feet. "Dibs on first shower," she said lamely.

Curving his fingers into a tight fist, he rolled his knuckles against his thigh. When he opened his mouth to speak, Camille darted through the cabin door before he had the chance. Better to feel the hollow ache of cowardliness than face another painful argument about an affair that never should've happened in the first place.

Lighter and smaller than the ferry, the *Sea Dreamin'* beat the *Puerto Azul* to Mazatlán by several hours, arriving at the public dock around seven in the morning. Camille watched the yacht dock from the porthole above the chair she'd slept in. Aaron sat cross-legged on the bed, fully dressed, staring at the wall.

"Ready?" Camille asked.

He glanced sideways at her and gave a curt nod. "Let's get to work."

Like the ferry terminal in La Paz, the landing in Mazatlán boasted the repugnant stench of fishiness and gasoline, but as Mazatlán was a major tourist destination, the landing was at least double the size of La Paz and opened onto a pedestrian-friendly boardwalk that boasted an endless string of trinket shops, restaurants and motels.

Not knowing if the truck would be greeted by a cartel welcoming committee, they tucked into a narrow alley fifty yards from the still-empty ferry terminal and scanned the surrounding area for anything suspicious.

"Two men sitting in a parked car on the north end of the boardwalk," Aaron said under his breath.

Camille followed his gaze. The car in question was angled toward the ferry terminal. The men inside didn't speak to each other. Both wore blazers despite the heat. Maybe to hide their firearms, would be Camille's guess. No doubt about it, she and Aaron couldn't discount the possibility of the Cortez Cartel's presence. There could be any number of men whose job it was to escort the delivery truck to its destination. They could be watching from windows or disguised as vendors.

"We can't get any closer without revealing our-selves," she whispered.

Aaron slid the pack from her shoulder and dropped it to the ground between her legs. "Then we try to look inconspicuous while we wait for the ferry to arrive." Before she could protest, he snaked an arm around her waist and rolled to pin her against the alley wall with his body, dipping his face close to hers. "No one will pay us any mind if we seem otherwise occupied, and once the truck disappears into the city, all the eyes watch-ing it will follow. Then we'll find a hotel room for the night."

It was a solid plan, even if Aaron's nearness aroused in her a dizzying, if unwanted, desire. As they waited, Camille fought to think of any-thing except Aaron, the solid heat of his body ra-diating against hers, the perspiration gathering between them, the rise and fall of their chests in time with each other.

Just when Camille feared she might combust if he touched her a moment longer, the ferry appeared on the horizon. Once it had docked, the cartel truck was among the first vehicles to exit. It made a right turn onto the frontage road lining the boardwalk. The suspicious car pulled away from its parking spot and followed.

They held their position until the ferry had emptied of cars and people and traffic died down, then Aaron pushed from the wall and smoothed a hand over his sweat-drenched shirt. Camille took her first deep breath in over an hour and slung the backpack on her shoulder. After a final scan for danger, they slipped onto the sunny boardwalk and sought refuge in the nearest motel.

The desk clerk at the Hacienda del Playa Sur was happy to furnish them with a harbor-view room for only twenty more dollars a night than one looking out on the city. After weeks of sleeping in boats, room thirty-two seemed enormous.

While Aaron freshened up in the bathroom, she tucked the backpack with the tracking device into the deepest dresser drawer along with the guns and gazed solemnly at the comfortable-looking queen-size bed. She hadn't slept in a bed since the night before her birthday in her continuing effort to keep her distance from Aaron. But, man, did this bed beckon to her today.

With a bracing sigh, she wrenched her gaze from the bed and settled near the window with binoculars to scope out the area, painfully aware that she and Aaron had nothing left to do but wait in the room together until the following afternoon's ferry departure.

By that evening, the room that had seemed so enormous on first arrival had shrunk to a shoebox. Restless with nerves, they went over the strategy for the following day and checked the weapons. Aaron called his ICE team, then Camille phoned her boss with an update. After that, they were back to square one.

When they bumped into each other the second time while prowling aimlessly around the room, Aaron laughed. "That's enough. I'm ordering dinner."

Aaron conversed in Spanish with someone on

the hotel's phone. Camille slipped into the bathroom, ready for a long, hot shower to give her a needed break from being too close to Aaron.

When she emerged, her skin pink from the hot water, her hair damp, Aaron had two place settings arranged on the room's small round table. The mouthwatering smell of garlic and peppers tempted her nose. With a boyishly anxious expression, he presented the setup with a wave of his hand.

"This is the closest I can get to taking you out on a proper date."

Camille froze in the bathroom doorway. *Oh, no...*

"Wine?" he asked, gesturing to a bottle on the table.

"Aaron, no. I—"

He shrugged and pulled out a chair. "Save it, Camille. Have a seat."

The food did smell amazing. And she could really use a drink to settle her nerves. Besides, what was her alternative plan? To hide in the bathroom until Aaron went to sleep? Even she wasn't that big of a coward. Tentatively, she settled into the chair. Aaron pushed a plastic cup toward her and kept his eyes on her while she drank deeply.

On such an empty stomach as she had, she felt the relaxing effects of the alcohol in no time flat. Before she knew it, she was laughing at Aaron's jokes and digging into her hearty plate of chicken, beans and a sweet-corn tamale.

Over a second round of wine, they talked about their lives growing up. Camille felt compelled to share stories with him she'd never revealed to any-one else, even her sister. And she'd laughed more than she had in years.

When their plates and the wine bottle were empty, Aaron stood and flicked on the clock radio. A slow guitar song floated through the air. Aaron offered her his hand. "Shall we dance?"

Camille's gut clenched. "No, thank you. I'm awful. Really, it's not my thing."

"But it's mine." He bent until his nose brushed

her cheek and whispered, "Let me dance with you, Camille. There's no one here but us."

She knew the wine was to blame, but nevertheless, she found herself taking his hand. "Just one dance."

He pulled her near and kept her there with a hand pressed to the small of her back. To her surprise, relaxing into his lead came naturally to her. For the first time in her life, she enjoyed dancing. She nestled into his neck, relishing the way his stubble grazed her cheek. She inhaled and was overcome by his intoxicating scent. It was a bitter memory that she once thought he smelled of clean laundry—pristine and simple, full of sunshine and golden happiness. Now she knew better.

This was the scent of the man who carried her when she could barely move for the pain in her leg, the scent that wrapped around her each night with the promise of safekeeping until dawn. This scent was her partner, matching her every movement throughout each dangerous step of their mission. It was the heady blend of sweat, soap and maleness swirled with the spice of him that she tasted when he kissed her.

She had never needed anything or anyone as much as she needed this man.

And, in her fear, she was wasting what precious time they had left together. What a fool she was not to savor every second she had with Aaron before she lost him to the world. She stroked his jaw and ran the pad of her thumb across his lower lip.

Aaron's arms tightened around her. He angled his head to study her face, his expression guarded. She couldn't blame him for that. She'd done an ace job of pushing him away.

She poured her need into a hungry look. "Kiss me. Please."

His hands crept to either side of her face, locking her in place as his lips descended. He froze an inch away. "If I kiss you, we're taking it all the way." His voice verged on angry. "Tomorrow morning, I wake up with you in my arms. No regrets, no picking a fight this time. You get in bed with me tonight, you're staying there."

She studied the severity of his features, marveling at the way intimacy brought out the darkest aspects of his personality. Determined to lighten the mood, she quirked an eyebrow at him and nodded toward the bed. "Think we'll make it all the way to the bed?"

His smile was ruthless. "Eventually."

Chapter 14

Camille allowed Aaron to back her into the wall with a blazing kiss. He loved the way she wrapped a leg around his waist, cradling his hardness between her thighs. He pressed into her, and she answered by rotating her hips, stroking him—a move he felt all the way to his toes.

With a groan of blissful agony, he broke from her mouth to kiss a trail down her throat, pausing with his lips over her pulse point, feeling the pounding of her heart. "Oh, baby. What I want to do to you…"

"What *you* want to do to me?" she teased, reaching between them to unsnap the top button of his jeans. "What about what *I* want to do to you?"

He rose and looked into her vivid green eyes, brushing her lower lip with his thumb. She really didn't get it yet, did she? The depth of his love for her. "You've already done it, Camille."

Inhaling sharply, she tucked her chin, averting her gaze. One day soon, he'd push the issue of their future, but for tonight, making love to her was enough. After brushing a kiss across her temple, he dropped his hands from her face and pushed her pants and panties down, then divested her of her shirt and bra.

He slid a hand behind the small of her back, arching her chest up as though in offering to him, and captured a nipple between his lips. He teased it into a taut point, then suckled it between his teeth. Camille moaned and wound her leg around him.

"I love the way your skin tastes," he murmured. "I need more."

He swept her off her feet and set her atop the

dresser. Beginning at her ankles, he kissed the inside of her leg all the way up. She braced her hands in his hair with the first stroke of his tongue on her folds. His name rolled from her lips, over and over, a plea and a prayer. The most exquisite sound he'd ever heard, raw and real and full of the love she was so scared to admit. He reached up her side and twined his fingers with hers as she tipped over the edge with the sharp cry of release.

He stood, licking the wetness from his lips, the need to be inside her stringing him as tight as a rubber band stretched beyond its limits. Out of habit, he reached for the wallet in his back pocket, trembling with the need to get a condom on and surge into Camille's body, but his hand only found the cheap, canvas wallet he'd bought at the corner store their first night in La Paz.

Then it hit him. The box of condoms he'd purchased on the sly the day after he decided to seduce her was tucked in the yacht's dresser— unopened. The night he and Camille made love, using protection hadn't once crossed his mind.

He'd never forgotten before, not in the seventeen years since losing his virginity. Then again, he'd never felt as crazy in love or as crazy with need as he had that night on the boat. All he'd wanted was to make her his in a permanent, tangible way. Well, mission accomplished.

For all either of them knew, Camille could be pregnant.

He stared in wide-eyed wonder at her gorgeous body, open and wet—ready for him. And maybe, miraculously, carrying his child. He braced his hands against the dresser on either side of her thighs. "Camille, the first time…we didn't use protection."

The calm strength on her face sent a fresh wave of surprise through his body. This wasn't news to her.

"I know," she whispered, dragging a finger along his tensed jaw. "It's okay."

"I don't have a condom tonight either." Impossibly hard and trembling with barely leashed control, he waited for her response to his unspoken question, not trusting himself to even brush her leg before she granted him permission to proceed. If she told him to stop, to wait until a different night when they were more prepared—God help him—he'd bow to her wishes. They had a lifetime to explore each other's bodies, and that knowledge might have to be enough to sustain him tonight.

Hurt flashed in her eyes. Nodding, she sat back, folding her arms over her breasts. "You want to stop. All right."

Slipping his fingers into her clenched fists, he tugged her arms away from her body and held her hands in his. "Oh, baby, it's not like that. I'm all in. This is your choice."

Gradually, her fingers relaxed in his grip and the worry lines on her forehead eased. She met his gaze, her expression no longer hurt, but stubborn. "I'm not scared of the future anymore, not like I once was." She reached a hand between them, her fingernails rasping against his stomach, and grasped his erection, stroking it to full hardness. "I want this. I want you."

Seizing hold of her hips, he pulled her toward him until the tip of his hardness nestled at the entrance of her body. "You have me, Camille." His voice, low and raw, surprised him. He sounded as desperate as he felt.

With his hands under her hips, he surged into her. She met his challenging pace, demanding it as hard as he was willing to give. When she opened her mouth in a moan, he claimed it with his tongue, wondering if she tasted the lingering spice of her arousal on his lips, as he did.

The moment he felt his release building, he slowed the rhythm of his thrusts and reached a hand between them. As his fingers worked, he dived into the skin of her neck with his teeth and lips until she tensed and stopped breathing. Then she shattered with violent intensity around him. He moved his hand to her hips and thrust deeply into her pulsing core. With a guttural sound, he spilled himself into her.

Wrapping her tightly in his arms, he lowered his head to her shoulder, breathing hard, reveling in the feel of their bodies joined together. She clung to him, locking her ankles around his waist, squeezing his still-pulsing erection inside her. He knew, unequivocally, that he'd never let her go.

By midday on Monday, they were in final stages of preparation to board the four o'clock ferry. Once they confirmed that the cartel truck had embarked, Aaron walked to the terminal to purchase tickets. Camille stayed behind to prep their weapons and perform a final check of the tracking device and explosives.

As she strapped on her ankle holster, Aaron walked through the hotel room door. "I love it when you go into warrior mode." He smacked her backside. "It's sexy as hell. Maybe you can wear that to bed sometime."

She smiled indulgently, relieved that his playful side had returned in full force. Anything but the intense, dead-serious man he became during sex. "Do you have our tickets?"

"Yep. Had to double the bribe I wanted to pay to the ticket guy, but it's done."

Camille hoisted her backpack onto her shoulder. "Let's get to work."

Camille and Aaron boarded the ferry with at least fifty other people. They each wore hats and black shirts they'd picked up that morning, all with tourist slogans, and sunglasses. Camille carried the backpack with the tracking device wrapped in a change of clothes, should she need a fresh disguise. Aaron had a backpack, too, with a change of clothes, a flashlight and duct tape, among other items.

Another bribe gained them entry without passports to validate the names on their tickets. Once past the ticket taker, they descended the stairs to the auto level and slipped to a section packed tightly with vehicles whose drivers had already left for the upper decks. The cartel delivery truck sat sandwiched between an RV and a minivan near the center of the boat.

The smell, a heady blend of gasoline and car exhaust, was nauseating. Camille breathed through her mouth but was supremely annoyed by the distracting urge to throw up.

Aaron tested each door they passed until he found one unlocked. They hustled into the backseat of a tiny, rusted gray car in case the ferry personnel did a final check that the level was cleared of people before locking it for the journey. Aaron lay on the floor of the car and Camille dropped on top of him. There they waited, embracing tightly, two bundles of white-hot nerves.

They heard their entombment one sound at a time, each echoing through the cavernous chamber with unmistakable clarity—the gears grinding as the ramp lifted, the clunk of the light switch turning off followed by the receding hum of the fluorescent bulbs into silence, the stairwell door sealing with a dull thud and, finally, the turn of the lock.

The rumble of the ferry motor rose to a roar. Low haunting moans and creaks told them the ship had started its trip across the sea.

Camille rose, blinking and looking around, waiting for her eyes to adjust. It was disorienting to realize there would be no adjustment—there wasn't even the barest hint of light for her eyes to filter. She grabbed her backpack, opened the door and stepped into the darkness.

Aaron emerged behind her and shut the door. Camille cringed as the sound reverberated around them, even though she knew there was no logical reason to be stealthy. They were alone.

Not far away, a second car door shut. Aaron's arms stiffened around Camille. A man cleared his throat. The faint light of a cell phone reflected off car windows two aisles over. They stood frozen, listening as the man, in heavily accented English, spoke the words running through Camille's head.

"Someone else is here."

It was probably a stowaway, someone too cheap to pay the price of a ferry ticket, someone like them who had hidden until the coast was clear. Just because Camille and Aaron lived in constant awareness of danger didn't mean the rest of the world operated that way, too.

Hard-soled boots tapped a steady, unhurried pace along the floor, growing louder and closer. A flashlight flipped on, scanning over the cars like a floodlight at a prison sweeps the exercise yard at night. Camille and Aaron ducked, hunching next to the car door. This was no stowaway.

Maybe the ferry company kept a security officer with the autos to guard against vandalism. If that were the case, the risk to Camille and Aaron was potentially more substantial than being trapped overnight with a half dozen cartel thugs. They were in the country illegally and each was packing multiple weapons…including enough dynamite to sink the ferry.

Whether they were dealing with ferry security or the Cortez Cartel was immaterial at the moment, though. At the unmistakable *chink-chink* of a pump action shotgun cocking, Aaron dug his fingers into Camille's arm and pulled her under the car.

Camille lay rigidly next to Aaron, listening to the blood pounding under her skin in syncopated rhythm with the boots clicking toward them along the metal floor.

She tucked the pack with the tracking device against the inside of the car's rear tire, either hiding the evidence or keeping it safe for later—however the next critical minutes played out. When the light of the flashlight was bright enough for her to see Aaron's silhouette on the floor next to her, she nudged him, then scooted out the other side of the car into the aisle. Aaron followed.

They crouched in the shadows, their guns pointed at the ground, their eyes fixated on the flashlight as it swung left and right, searching. Though it threatened to expose them, the flashlight gave Aaron and Camille the upper hand. They knew precisely where their opponent was, his direction and speed, whereas he could have no idea how many people he was dealing with or where they were.

Because the vehicles were laid out in a grid of

even rows, Camille and Aaron's options were limited to either moving in the same direction as their pursuer—beating him to the rear wall of the auto level and potentially cornering themselves—or the opposite, which meant they had to walk right past the person searching for them.

Keeping low, Aaron stepped toward the light. It was the same choice Camille would have made. He kept the pace slow and steady. Camille moved lightly on the balls of her feet in a crouched position under the level of the car windows they passed.

When the light swept over the car they were behind, they molded themselves against the tires until the beam passed over the tops of their heads. They continued moving until they stood on the opposite side of a small pickup truck from the person searching for them.

Peering through the truck windows, they were finally able to size up their opponent—a single man, tall and bulky. It was impossible to tell if he wore a security uniform or if he was a cartel operative, but he was indeed carrying a shotgun that he steadied by tucking under his arm. It was an odd choice of weapon because it required two hands to steady and fire. He would have to either drop the flashlight or hold it in his mouth to shoot accurately.

Camille's confidence blossomed. They could get this guy. Piece of cake.

After the man walked away from them, Aaron rose and jogged to the end of the aisle, Camille trailing him closely. When Aaron stopped, the rubber sole of his sneaker squeaked. They dropped to their stomachs next to the bumper of the first car on the row. Aaron cursed under his breath.

The flashlight beam grew erratic, waving wildly, then bobbing as the man trotted in their direction. Aaron unzipped his pack. Camille's eyes had adjusted enough to the dimness that she could make out the roll of tape and shirt he removed.

In the barest whisper, they hashed out the details of Aaron's plan. He shoved the shirt into his pocket, wore the tape like a bracelet and picked up his gun. "Let's move."

They sprinted across the aisle the man was running on and ducked behind the nearest car. There were several feet of space between that car and the motor home behind it. Camille crept behind Aaron into the shadow between the two vehicles, completely concealed behind the height of the motor home, and concentrated on the beam of light as it grew brighter. The *clip-clop* of the man's shoes grew louder, closer.

She withdrew a D-volt battery from her pocket, one of two she'd grabbed in case the flashlight ran out of juice. She threw it. It landed with a clink several cars in front of them. The beam of light swerved toward the noise as the man jogged nearer.

They waited until he passed them. Then they burst forth and slammed into him, crushing him against a car hood. Camille pressed her gun to his temple. There was no need to speak. He got her message loud and clear and raised his arms in surrender.

Aaron disarmed him and took the flashlight and cell phone. Their captive twisted around, trying to see who had accosted him, but Aaron was smart enough not to reveal their identities and shone the flashlight into the man's face. He jolted and closed his eyes against the brightness.

Aaron and Camille shared a questioning look. She didn't recognize the man. Could be a cartel operative, could be ferry security. Aaron tore a strip of tape and affixed it over the man's mouth. The T-shirt went over his head. He crossed the man's wrists behind him and secured them with tape.

They marched their captive to the old, gray beater they'd hidden in initially. Aaron shoved him into the front passenger seat and taped his still-blindfolded head and torso to the seatback, rendering him immobile from the waist up.

As an extra precaution, Camille snapped both the interior doorknobs off. Even if the guy managed to wiggle a hand free, he wouldn't be able to escape. The owner of the car would be in for a shock the next morning, but Camille and Aaron planned on being long gone by then—before whoever the man called on his cell phone had a chance to spot them.

She retrieved the pack from under the car and they worked their way to the delivery truck. They scooted along the ground on their backs until they were staring at the truck's filthy undercarriage. Aaron assumed flashlight duty while Camille searched for the perfect nook in the space between the frame and the floor of the truck bed, finding one such spot near the front wheel axle.

The explosives that had seemed unassuming as they sat in the pack felt volatile and deadly as she rested them on her chest. The dynamite sticks were bundled together with tape, then strapped to a 6-volt battery and topped with a cell-phone detonator and the tracking device. Once they'd secured Rosalia's safety, all Camille would need to do was dial that phone's number using the cell phone in her pocket and...*boom.*

Her hands, sweating and shaky with nerves, fumbled the duct tape Aaron handed her as she picked at its tacky edge, trying to get it started. Twice, she dropped it.

Aaron took the tape and pulled out a length. "We've got all night. Try to relax."

"There's dynamite sitting on my heart. I'm not going to relax."

"All right, then, let's get it over with."

Camille glanced sideways at him, then tucked the bomb above the axle. She wound the duct tape around the bomb and the frame over and over again until she was satisfied that no matter how many potholes the truck was bound to hit between the ferry terminal and the warehouse, the device wouldn't move or fall off.

Aaron jostled the device a bit to double-check her handiwork. "That's good enough. Let's find someplace to crash for the rest of the night."

He helped Camille up and used the flashlight

to check on their captive, who had remained silent and unmoving in the car. He led the way to a pickup truck that gave them a clear view of the man should they point a beam of light his direction. Camille stepped over various tools and ropes in the truck bed and sat against the cab. Aaron settled next to her and slung an arm around her shoulders.

In less time than she would have liked, the flashlight flickered and dimmed, then went out. In the darkness, Camille and Aaron instinctively pulled closer together.

"I don't think we should use our other flashlight, especially since we don't have enough backup batteries anymore," he said. "It's going to be a long night and who knows why we might need them later."

"You're right. Good call."

Camille had never feared darkness. But here, in the guts of a rusty ship amid cars lined up like metal caskets, with the stomach-turning stench of car exhaust and the ghostly creaking of the ship joints, it took her only a few minutes to realize how terrible this journey would have been without Aaron. The weight of his arm around her, his fingers entwined with hers, gave her the strength to keep the shadows at bay.

He pushed his watch light on and checked the time. "Only fifteen hours to go. Wanna make out?" He planted a kiss on her nose. "Oops, missed your mouth. Let me try again."

He groped her face with his fingers, pretending he couldn't find her lips. When he poked her in the ear, Camille smiled in spite of herself.

"Aha," he exclaimed, pretending to find her mouth. She felt the smile on his lips when he kissed her, as though he found himself highly amusing.

"You're a silly man."

"Yes, but you secretly love that about me."

She started to chuckle, but panic, sudden and violent, hit her like a sucker punch to her gut. She struggled for composure, but her brain was spinning so fast out of control that she feared she might pass out.

"Camille, are you all right?"

"I'm fine. Just tired."

But she wasn't fine, and the pain had only just begun. Planting a tracking device and staging a dangerous rescue was a piece of cake compared to this. Oh, God, she really did have the worst luck in the world. Her whole damn life was one big cautionary tale.

At some point, and she wasn't sure when because she hadn't been paying close enough attention, she'd let her guard down. She knew better than to get emotional about her affair with a man who treated casual sex like a hobby, yet she'd done it anyway.

She'd fallen madly, eternally, head over heels in love with Aaron Montgomery.

She drew a silent gasp, desperate for air as an involuntary shiver rattled her spine.

Before he'd shone his bright light into her life, she lived as if alone on a distant, dark planet.

When they first met, she found his good humor threatening, as though levity were a sign of weakness. It took two years and being taken hostage by a drug cartel, but Camille finally realized the immeasurable value of Aaron's optimism. She had no idea how she would survive without him.

When they took down Rodrigo Perez and their mission was over, her plan was to go on a grand adventure. She was supposed to figure out what made her happy. What if she knew what made her happy, but he wasn't hers to keep?

Registering her agitation, Aaron hauled her onto his lap. "You're shaking like a leaf. Are you sure you're okay?"

She huffed. "I guess I have to be."

"Do you think you could sleep? I'll watch over you." He pressed her head to his chest and stroked her hair.

His touch hurt. His ever-present chivalry hurt. She squeezed her eyes shut. She should push him away, start weaning herself from her dependence on him. Impossible. The weakling that she was, she'd cling to the brightest light in her life until she was forced back into the darkness.

That he would leave her was a given. She had nothing to hold him to her, no argument that could convince him to give her a chance. What was she supposed to say? *I'm broken and pessimistic and awkward, but love me anyway. I have no career, no prospects, nothing to offer you but my sorry self...but I need you. You're the only thing in this world that makes me happy. Maybe you would be happy with me, too.*

Yeah, right.

Yet even though they would go separate ways after their mission, their connections to Juliana and Jacob would link them forever. Aaron would always be in her life, at barbecues and birthday parties, weddings and funerals. She would have to endure the sight of him flirting and dancing. It had been painful enough watching him with other women before she realized she loved him.

Someday, maybe she'd be able to watch him

with detached fondness, remembering the adventure they shared in Mexico.

Someday, maybe.

For now, though, it was time to figuratively smack some sense into herself. Once she rescued Rosalia, she'd have a lifetime to feel the heartache that came with loving the wrong person and watching him walk away. Until then, she had work to do.

She reached into her pocket and fingered the cell phone that was the key to finding Rosalia. To drown out the sounds and odor of the ferry, she tucked her face under Aaron's chin. She drank in his fresh, familiar scent and let his heartbeat lull her to sleep.

Aaron woke Camille as soon as the heavy metal door to the auto level opened. Grabbing their packs, they slunk over the side of the pickup and behind a motor home, where they stood until car owners filed in around them.

Camille's heart pounded against her ribs and

her hands shook with adrenaline and stress as she thought about the next few critical minutes. They had to make it past the commercial port's armed guards and into a taxi. Not to mention the fact that the man they'd captured had tipped someone off over the phone about the presence of people in the auto level. She just prayed that whoever it was wasn't waiting to ambush them the minute they stepped off the boat.

Aaron rummaged through his backpack with a concerned look on his face, muttering about how he couldn't find his cell phone. Under the pretense that he left it in their cabin, they pushed through the throng of people pouring onto the auto level and up two flights of stairs to the pedestrian exit ramp.

They kept their heads down, walking fast. Camille could see a line of waiting taxis on the other side of the chain-link fence surrounding the port, past two armed security guards. Fifty yards to relative safety.

She scanned the crowd on the dock. No black

sedans in sight, no Perez. No thug-looking cartel types at all, only families and businessmen, truckers and vacationers. They had this. They skirted a slow-moving family on the ramp and tucked behind a tall, overweight man.

The exit ramp gave way to solid ground. Camille and Aaron stayed with the crowd moving toward the exit. Only twenty yards to the taxis.

Holding her breath, she kept her face on her feet as she crossed paths with the guards. No one stopped her or Aaron. Aiming at a tiny, white hatchback taxi, she hastened her steps. Aaron outpaced her and piled into the backseat first to give directions to the driver in Spanish. Camille tugged her door, but something kept it from closing.

She looked up to see the barrel of a pistol in her face.

Carlos "Two Down" Reyes sat beside her, sneering as he shoved the gun against Camille's throat. A second man dropped into the front passenger seat, a gun trained on the driver, who put the car in gear and started down the road in the opposite direction from La Paz. Camille clutched Aaron's hand.

Two Down gave a wheezy laugh and ground the gun into her skin. "Let me guess, *señorita*. You're the brains and he's the brawn of your little operation?"

"Wrong, dimwit," Aaron answered. "She's the brains and the brawn. I'm just the arm candy."

She glanced sideways at him and saw that his door hadn't latched and he held it steady with his other hand. A plan took root in her mind. It wasn't perfectly thought out, but it might be their only hope.

She waited until Two Down started chattering in Spanish to the man in the front passenger seat. Slowly she reached into her pocket for the cellphone detonator and the scrap of paper with the code and transferred them to Aaron's hand.

His eyes grew questioning as he tucked the items into his jacket pocket.

"I know you'll come for me," she said in the barest whisper.

"What?"

The taxi slowed to maneuver over a speed bump.

"This is the only way," she said. She lunged at Two Down, deflecting his gun as she pushed Aaron out of the car with her feet. "Drive," she shouted at the driver. He stepped on the gas. Camille pulled Aaron's door shut as Two Down's gun connected with the top of her skull. She fought against unconsciousness, but a second blow landed on her head and she was out.

Chapter 15

Aaron inspected the bloody road rash on his arm in the yacht's bathroom mirror. "Dreyer? Montgomery."

"Did something go wrong when you planted the tracking device?"

"Device is in place, but Fisher's been taken." What he didn't bother to mention was that Camille finally managed to martyr herself. Stubborn, stubborn woman. If those men laid a hand on her, he'd blow the entire Baja Peninsula out of the water. "Patch me through to Santero. We're going in tonight."

"Fisher was kidnapped again by the Cortez Cartel? Are you sure?"

Aaron picked a bit of blacktop out of his skin and slammed it into the sink. "Do I sound confused?" He bit back the rest of the rant on the tip of his tongue, remembering too late that he was speaking to his superior.

"No, you don't. Take a breath, Montgomery. Flying off the handle isn't going to save her."

He scrubbed a hand over his mouth. "I know that, sir. But going after her as soon as humanly possible will."

"Roger that. I'll contact Santero and green-light his team."

"I want to be a part of her rescue."

"That's not a good idea," Dreyer said. "You're too emotionally invested for a matter this delicate."

Aaron sucked in a breath through gritted teeth. "She threw herself at the cartel so I could escape." *And she's the love of my life.* "I need to help get her back. Please."

Dreyer was silent for a beat. "We can't take a chance of this line being tapped or you being followed, so I'll have someone pick you up in four hours and bring you to ICE's secure location within the city."

"Thank you, sir."

He rattled off the first location that came to mind for a rendezvous point, then ended the call and looked at the bed he'd shared with Camille and the bathroom where he'd cut her hair. This would be the last time he saw the *Happily Ever After*. No matter what happened tonight with the rescue, he wouldn't be back.

He grabbed a backpack and tossed in the binder of ICE intel and the rest of the cash and weapons. He dumped the contents of the dresser drawers on the bed, checking for anything he might need or any incriminating evidence of their time there. Out tumbled the box of condoms.

With a huff, he picked it up and sat on the bed.

Funny how life was. In the past few weeks, he'd done and experienced terrible things. And yet, in

Camille's arms, he'd found his life's purpose—to be accountable to and cherished by a woman. This one particular woman. All his years in pursuit of amusement—years of fast women, fast cars and fast sports—had been ineffective attempts to stave off the emptiness that came with a lack of purpose. Camille had given his life substance. She made him invincible.

And she was gone.

He set the box aside. The possibility of having a baby with the woman he loved was wonderful and terrifying, but hardly pertinent. Camille's life was in danger, if she wasn't dead already.

Please, God, don't let her be dead.

He flipped on the tracking device locator and watched a red blip on the map a good ten miles or more southeast of La Paz. The delivery truck had reached its destination. The only question was, had Camille been taken to the same place? Only one way to find out.

He slung the backpack over his shoulder and strode from the room. Knowing he'd go insane if he stayed stationary until the rendezvous, he decided to perform some preliminary surveillance.

Following the GPS coordinates from the tracking device along the road southeast of La Paz, he drove past the ferry terminal. The dirt roads became crude, the homes more dilapidated and sparse until there were no homes at all but endless miles of shrub and cacti-covered foothills.

Over a half hour southeast of the city, twenty estates rose up from the desolation and lined the mouth of the bay. Thick, barbed wire-topped walls of brick and plaster standing ten feet tall separated the properties from each other and the road. In case the cartel stronghold was located here, Aaron kept his distance. No need to tip off any guards to his presence.

The tracking device transmitted from within the fourth property to the right. Set far back from the gate was a massive two-story mansion. He doubted Rodrigo Perez could afford such luxury. This place had to belong to Alejandro Milán.

The entrance gate was a solid sheet of dark iron

topped by as much barbed wire as the fence line. At least from the front and sides, the estate was impenetrable. Hopefully Milán wasn't as meticulous about the security of his backyard.

In a text to Dreyer, he entered the GPS coordinates and requested satellite photos. After using the phone to snap pictures of the entrance gate, he watched for signs of activity until the rendezvous time approached, but all was quiet. As he waited and watched, his thoughts slid to his last moments with Camille and the expression of courage and resolve on her face as she shoved him from the cab.

She was incomparable to any person he'd ever known—and he'd destroy any man who hurt her.

With a final glare at Milán's entrance gate, he retraced his route to the city, through the cobblestone side streets of downtown and up a steep grade into a suburban neighborhood, past the Gigante Market. A glance at his watch told him he had thirty minutes to spare. On a whim, he made a right turn on to Ana's street.

Her car was parked curbside. He idled the bike half a block down and observed the quiet street. He might be connecting dots that weren't there, but his instincts kept niggling at him that somehow Ana was involved with the cartel. He and Camille had too many run-ins with them while in contact with her. On the other hand, if she had an allegiance to Alejandro Milán or Rodrigo Perez, she could have killed them the night they stayed at her house.

A hand touched his shoulder. Drawing his 9 mm, he twisted toward it.

Ana stood next to him, flanked by three huge men holding firearms inside the flaps of their jackets.

"Aaron, what a wonderful surprise." She sounded pleasant and not at all rattled to be standing at gunpoint.

Aaron held his aim. "Who are they?"

"This is my brother, Ramón." She gestured to the most sharply dressed man of the three who looked to be in his early forties. "And these are a couple of our…friends. They are in town on business."

He tried to play it cool, but the proliferation of firepower made it a tough sell. "Nice to meet you all. How have you been, Ana?"

She indulged in a throaty chuckle, but she was only a facsimile of the sexy teacher who had sheltered them for a night. The inhumanity exuding from her now made Aaron's mouth go dry. It was either divine intervention or blind luck she hadn't murdered them when she had the chance. "I'm well. How is Camille?"

Something about the way she asked set Aaron's teeth on edge. Maybe it was the slight quirk of a smug grin on her lips or the blade-sharp glint in her eyes. But he was certain she knew Camille had been recaptured.

"She's fine."

Ana's eyes narrowed the tiniest bit. "I'm sure she is. What are you doing outside my apartment, waving a gun in my face?"

He held the gun steady. "I was in the neighbor-hood."

"How convenient for me. Shall we go inside before we're all arrested for carrying illegal fire-arms?"

"Sweet of you to offer, but I'm late for a meet-ing. I'll see you around."

Her brother and the other men pulled their guns out of their jackets and aimed at Aaron's chest. Aaron thought about the arsenal stashed in his backpack, but he'd never have time to even pull the pin on a grenade before the three men shot him.

"I wasn't offering you a choice," she said.

One of the men plucked Aaron's gun from his hand. The other dragged him off the bike and frisked him. Ramón relieved him of the backpack. He was pushed along behind Ana up the stairs to her apartment, with Ramón and the others pull-ing up the rear of the procession.

"Tell me," Aaron said as they walked. "Do you work for Rodrigo Perez?"

"Oh, God, no. Ramón works for my father, Antonio Vega."

Nothing Ana could've said would have surprised Aaron more. They reached the apartment and he gaped at her as the hulking men shoved him inside. Ramón entered last and closed the door.

"You're related to Gael Vega?" Aaron whispered in disbelief. "You're with the La Mérida Cartel?"

She perched on the arm of the sofa and gestured for Aaron to sit in a chair. "Very good. Gael is my uncle. Since he was arrested, there has been quite a jostling for control. If my brother and I can deliver La Paz to our father, he will gain my uncle's approval as his replacement and we will become the most powerful family in Mexico."

"I assumed you were behind the Cortez Cartel's ambush of Camille at the supermarket. But you're part of the La Mérida Cartel," Aaron said.

"La Paz is about to become La Mérida's most important territory. Why dirty our hands ridding it of nosy American law enforcement when Perez wants you dead, too? I tipped off his men anonymously."

Aaron pulled his face in surprise. "Why kill us? We were doing all the dirty work for you."

"Yes. It is true that Milán's stronghold in La Paz made it too risky for our family to move in. But you and Camille have been extremely helpful. As soon as I realized that, I sat back and enjoyed the show."

The mention of the reclusive cartel boss threw Aaron for another loop. "Is Milán here, in La Paz?"

Ramón laughed. "Not for long."

Ana ignored her brother. "With so many of his men murdered in the past few weeks, Milán's not happy with Rodrigo Perez. He flew in yesterday to handle the mess and has recalled Perez and his men to his estate, making this the perfect opportunity for us to relieve them all of their power."

Aaron swallowed hard. The only way he understood cartels to oust each other from power was through vicious, indiscriminate bloodshed. "His estate is southeast of La Paz?"

"Yes. At least until we blow it up tonight."

Oh, no. "Wait," he croaked. "I have a counter-offer."

Ana looked amused. "That's sweet, Aaron. But like Milán, you have outlived your usefulness."

Ramón shoved the butt of his gun in Aaron's ribs and hoisted him onto his feet.

No. He couldn't die now, not when he was so close to saving Camille, not when his death would destroy her chance of rescue tonight by the ICE unit. Pulling his arm from Ramón's grip, he squared his shoulders. "I disagree. Why not let me finish the job by taking down Milán and Perez? It's no risk to your family to let me try. If the Cortez Cartel kills me in the process, your hands are still clean."

"I'm not sure I see how that would be worthwhile for me and my family."

"Look, if you blow up Milán's estate tonight, you'll kill Camille—a decorated law enforcement officer—and Rodrigo Perez's kidnapped daughter who's an American citizen. I've already notified my bosses about Camille's recapture at Milán's property. And I've already notified them about you, Ana. If you kill me, Camille and Perez's daughter, you'll bring the wrath of the entire Unites States law enforcement down on the La Mérida Cartel. You know I'm right. Do you think your uncle will allow your father to lead the family after that?"

Judging by the clench of her jaw and the white of her knuckles, she heard his message loud and clear.

She placed a hand on Ramón's wrist and he lowered his weapon. Crossing her arms over her chest, she studied Aaron. "How long do you need?"

Aaron's heart pounded as his hope blossomed. "One day, that's all. Give me one day and I'll hand you the keys to the city."

With a nod, she opened her front door and held his backpack out to him. "One day. And if you fail, you and your precious Camille won't live to see day two." She ran her tongue over her lower lip. "Get out of here before I change my mind."

Chapter 16

Aaron did a quick roll call with the three fire-arms he'd concealed on his person for his meeting with Santero. No doubt about it, he trusted the guy, but stalking through the alleyways of La Paz at dusk carried its own inherent risks. And the confrontation with Ana had rattled him to the core. He would not be caught off guard again.

Unlike the last time he'd come to this abandoned, half-constructed building, tonight he wheeled the dirt bike inside and propped it along the wall, out of sight from the road. Santero hadn't arrived, which gave Aaron too much time to think. Too much time to remember. But, then, what had he expected, choosing this building as a rendez-vous point?

He crouched along the far wall and smoothed a hand over the smear of dry blood. First time he'd ever stripped Camille of her clothes had been in this very spot, when he'd thought the blood saturating her jacket and shirt had been hers.

"Jesus Christ," came a harsh whisper from the alley. Aaron whirled, drawing his gun. "You better be in there, Montgomery, because a rat the size of a freakin' dog just ran over my foot."

"I'm here."

Through the doorway walked a lean-muscled, scowling Latino man about Aaron's age.

"Diego Santero?" Aaron asked.

"In the flesh. You gonna shoot me?"

Aaron tucked the gun in his waistband. "Sorry. I'm a little on edge."

"Maybe it's this creepy place you picked for a meeting. Is that blood on the wall?"

"You said to choose somewhere quiet, and I

know firsthand a person could spend hours here without drawing notice."

Santero held his hands up in mock surrender. "I'm just saying. The ambience sucks."

"My partner's been kidnapped, so excuse me if I don't give a damn about ambience."

Santero sniffed and stalked to the window, sinking his weight into his arms on the ledge as he stared at the alley outside. "Here's the deal. When those federal stiffs asked me to share my operation with Mr. Desert ICE himself, I nearly peed my pants laughing. I never share control of my jobs. You got that?" He pushed from the window and glared at Aaron.

"Absolutely." He got it, all right, but was having trouble syncing the image he'd formed in his head about a Latin-American agent named Diego Santero and the hostile, Jersey-accent-sporting jerk who'd shown up. "By federal stiffs, you mean Dreyer?"

"Freakin' Dreyer. He has the personality of drywall. The man talks like he's got his butt cheeks clenched all the time. What a piece of work."

"He's your boss." Probably the wrong thing to say because Santero got up in his face real quick.

"You got a problem with my opinion already, Montgomery? You want to get into it right here in the middle of this rathole?"

Yikes. Aaron flexed his fingers, squelching the urge to punch Santero in the jaw. "Nope."

"This is my extraction job," Santero continued, backing off. "I call the shots. You want to play like you're a real ICE agent, fine. But you'd better keep a cool head because if your bleeding heart interferes with me doing my job, you're out. Understood?"

Aaron wasn't the one blowing his top at the moment, but he wasn't going to point that out. "I'm good. Let's roll."

As if he had his mood on some sort of switch, Santero's face softened. He slapped Aaron on the back. Maybe the anger had been an act to test

Aaron's ability to keep his emotions in check. "We'll ditch your bike, take my van."

Aaron nodded and started for the door.

"One more thing, Montgomery." He waited for Aaron to stop and look at him. "We're going to get her back. That's my job. And I'm really, really good at it."

Diego pulled into the garage of a ramshackle house on the western edge of the city. The place didn't look much like a covert ops war room, but while in Mexico, Aaron had learned the hard way that nothing—and no one, for that matter—could be taken at face value.

They entered the house through a door in the garage. The front room was full of dusty furniture, the curtain wide open to the street out front. Behind the wall separating the front room from the kitchen, out of view from the exposed window, Thomas Dreyer stood in front of a room full of high-tech computer equipment.

Aaron recovered from the shock of seeing his

boss and shook Dreyer's hand. "Didn't realize you were going to be here, sir."

Dreyer afforded him a terse nod. "ICE agents always have each other's backs. That's the first rule you'll need to know now that you're on the job, Agent Montgomery."

Wait...did that mean... "You're bringing me on to the ICE unit?"

"Welcome to the Department of Homeland Security. Glad to have you aboard."

Santero coughed. "I think I threw up a little in my mouth, watching you two kiss each other's butts. Real freakin' heartwarming. How about we get on with the mission?" He stalked down a hallway.

Aaron followed. He'd suddenly been hired for his dream job, something he'd worked himself to the bone for the past year to achieve, and he felt nothing. Job titles, Santero's belligerence— none of it mattered until Camille was safe in his arms again. Then maybe, just maybe, he'd sock

Santero in the jaw like he wanted to and celebrate his new career.

In the middle of the back bedroom, four men and a woman leaned over a table covered in satellite photographs. A familiar face popped up, smiling. "Aaron!" Nicholas Wells strode over and shook his hand. "Good to see you alive and well, man."

"That would be thanks to Camille. She saved my hide more than once down here."

"Sounds like it's time to turn the tables and do a little saving of our own."

"Got that right. How'd you and Dreyer get down here so fast?"

Wells shrugged. "ICE sprung for the private jet, seeing as how we're going to bring down two cartel kingpins and rescue a missing child and a kidnapped police officer."

"Yeah, they're good like that."

Santero commanded the attention of the room. "Montgomery, you already know Wells. Here's the rest of my crew—Ryan Reitano, John Witter,

Rory Alderman and Alicia Troy. We've got two choppers standing by on a Navy vessel on the Pacific side of Baja. You've already been to the target property, but check out these satellite images we pulled about an hour ago. Sorriest security system I've ever seen."

From an aerial view, the Milán estate wasn't so much a fortress as an opulent mansion set close to the water and padded with thick tropical landscape. With its multiple balconies, brickwork and innumerable windows, the house would be simple enough to breach once they got past the gates and the guards. The backyard boasted a white sand beach and a private dock with three impressive boats tied to it—a yacht larger than the *Happily Ever After,* a motorboat built for speed and a mid-size fishing boat.

Troy tapped her finger on the photograph near the image of a huge, turquoise swimming pool. "Two armed guards are all we can pick out in the back. Two more in the front."

The white delivery truck sat in the circular

driveway on the property's west side. "There's enough space on the front driveway to chopper down," Aaron said.

Santero shook off the idea. "Not the right call for a hostage situation. If the tangos get wind of us, they could slit the hostages' throats before we cross the property line."

He tossed a photograph on top of the pile, the image zoomed back to encompass the landscape and water for a good ten miles in either direction, and pointed to the water edging the first property on the north side, four estates from their target. "We'll swim in from here. Once we've breached the shore, we'll follow the fence line of Milán's property to the foliage under the south-side balcony. From there, subduing the tangos will be as easy as plinking cows with a BB gun. To get in that position, though, we'll need a diversion for the guards."

Aaron took Camille's cell-phone detonator out of his pocket and set it on the table. "That, I can handle."

* * *

Camille woke in darkness. Lying prone on the hard ground, she rolled to her side with a wince. Her head was killing her.

The layer of crust on her lips tasted like blood. Not surprising.

She squirmed her way to a seated position with her back resting against the wall to take stock of the situation.

Damn. Once again she was a cartel hostage, imprisoned in an empty, cell-like room. This time, her hands had been bound in front of her with zip ties. This time, she was without Aaron or a rusty chair or even a window.

She was clothed, which was a bonus, because the air was cold and pungent with the smell of dirt. As if maybe she was in a basement…or a dungeon. She looked at the bare ceiling, made visible by the thin strip of light streaming under the door, and hissed through the pain when the back of her head hit the wall.

She'd done the right thing, pushing Aaron from

the taxi. If they'd both been captured, they'd both be trapped in this room with little hope of rescuing either themselves or Rosalia. If they'd both jumped from the car, the chance of one of them getting shot would've been too great. But with Aaron free, he could get help from the ICE unit standing by to rescue Rosalia, which was all that mattered to Camille. They could follow the tracking device to the cartel's stronghold, save the little girl and shut down the cartel.

Whether or not that's where Camille had been taken remained to be seen. Either way, sitting around waiting for help wasn't in her blood.

She tested the zip tie around her wrists. Made of heavy-duty nylon cable, it had been tightened to a snug fit that cut into her skin.

No problem.

She crawled to the thick metal door and listened for a sound of approach but heard none. Satisfied that she had at least a couple of minutes to work, she tucked her knee up close to her body and untied a shoelace.

One of the first lessons she'd learned as a Special Forces cop was of the innumerable benefits of paracord, the superstrong nylon rope used for parachutes and a million other tactical applications. Jacob taught her that the simplest way to guarantee a ready supply was to use it as shoelaces. Military-grade paracord wasn't sold at every corner store, especially in Mexico. But Walmart carried the next best thing, a braided polyester utility cord. She'd swapped both her and Aaron's regular laces for it—and thank goodness she had because it was about to break her out of prison.

Once she'd cleared the lace from the shoe, she tied simple loop knots at either end and secured one loop around her shoe. She threaded the cord through the zip tie, then slipped the second loop over her other shoe. Voilà. She had herself a genuine friction saw.

Rocking back to balance on her butt, she pedaled her feet in the air, moving the cable fast over the zip tie like a saw. It snapped within seconds.

With her ear to the door again, she listened. No sound. Excellent.

She made quick work of lacing her shoe and stood, turning in a slow circle. Now for the hard part. How the hell was she going to break free from a square cinder-block room with a solid metal door? She looked at the broken zip tie in her hand and had her answer.

Five minutes later, she'd finessed the lock open and eased into a dark, quiet hallway.

Voices filtered through the ceiling, adding evidence to her theory that she'd been locked in a basement. It'd be helpful to know for certain, but what she needed, more than anything, was a lethal weapon. At the moment, all she had at her disposal was the broken zip tie. While it had made a great lock pick, and would probably work well as a shiv, unless she was within striking distance of someone's artery or eye, she'd need to come up with something that packed a bigger punch.

Somewhere nearby, she heard a faint sneeze. A child's sneeze.

Step by quiet, deliberate step, she approached the nearest door and put her ear to it.

Minutes ticked by. The talking continued upstairs, but Camille was starting to wonder if perhaps it was a television.

She moved to the second door and listened. After a minute, something inside the room rustled. Then, with the voice of a little girl, the person in the room began to sing "Twinkle, Twinkle, Little Star."

Camille sagged with relief against the door. Rosalia. And she was alive and within her reach. She put her ear to the metal again to double-check that the girl was alone. The worst that could happen would be for her to walk in on Rosalia sitting with her father.

When she was certain Rosalia was alone, she turned the knob and pushed the door open.

Rosalia sat in the middle of a small bed covered in a faded yellow quilt. She had a doll in her hands and seemed to be making it dance to the song she sang. When she saw Camille, she startled.

"It's okay, Rosalia. I'm a friend of your mom."

Rosalia blinked up at her, considering. Camille closed the door and looked around. This room had no window either and was as cold as Camille's holding cell had been. A pile of clothes sat in one corner and a few toys lined the wall. A bucket sat near the door and one whiff told Camille it had been used as a toilet. At least the bastards had provided Rosalia with a bed.

"I remember you," Rosalia finally said. "From my papa's other house. Your hair's different now. It's brown like mine."

Camille sat on the bed. It wiggled as though the frame was barely holding together. "Yeah. My friend helped me with it."

"It's pretty."

She took the girl's hand and smiled. "Oh, Rosalia. I am so happy to see you. What do you say we find a way out of this place so I can get you back to your mommy?"

"Yes, please."

"Stand over by your clothes for a minute. I need to get something from under your bed."

With Rosalia out of the way, Camille wiggled a metal bar of the bed frame until it snapped off. Still not as effective as a gun, but a hundred times better than a zip tie. Despite that, she tucked the tie into her pocket. One never knew when a shiv might come in handy.

Fifty yards from shore, water slapped at Aaron's face as he treaded water in the Sea of Cortez alongside the rest of the ICE unit. The wet suit offered some protection, but even in Mexico's tropical climate, the winter sea was frigid and choppy. Hopefully he wouldn't need to fire his gun anytime soon because he was losing the fine motor functioning of his fingers.

They'd stopped one property over from their target to assess the situation.

Milán's backyard was decoratively lit, with each palm tree and flowering bush individually illuminated by spotlights on the ground. The windows of the house were dark with drawn drapes, save for one on the first floor, which glowed with the light of a television behind sheer white curtains.

The swimming pool threw its artificial blue-green light around the patio and lit the two guards from the bottom up, highlighting their legs, weapons and necks as they stood between the pool and the house, facing toward the sea. Their hands rested on rifles that hung at gut level in front of them.

Aaron's objective was to position himself along the dock between the yacht and the speedboat. Then he'd blow up the delivery truck.

When Santero gave the go-ahead signal, Aaron inhaled deeply and swam as fast as he could toward the boats. Though his lungs burned, he pushed himself to remain underwater until his arm hit the yacht. After another big breath, he submerged again and traced his way to the right, along the curve of the hull, until he hit the slimy underbelly of the dock between the two boats.

Santero had matched him stroke for stroke in

the water. As they'd agreed on, Dreyer, Wells and the rest of the team were farther back, behind the yacht.

Aaron slung the waterproof pack he'd carried onto the dock, but his fingers fumbled with the tiny zipper. Santero *tsk*ed impatiently. After a few clumsy attempts, Aaron shoved his fingers in his mouth to warm them. As soon as the painful sting of life returned to them, he tried again and this time, he succeeded.

He powered up the cell phone and dialed the numbers he'd memorized.

A deafening boom resounded all around them as a fireball belched into the sky, momentarily transforming night to day. Splinters of wood and debris rained over the house.

In sync with Santero, Aaron plunged underwater, swam under the dock and kept going all the way to the far edge of the property. He was aware of the rest of the team doing the same but kept his focus on moving through the water as fast as humanly possible.

A quick scan told him the guards had gone to investigate and the backyard was empty. On Santero's command, they swam ashore and sprinted into the shadows of the fence that ran along the side of the house. The air on land felt downright balmy against Aaron's face and hands compared to the water, and his limbs rapidly regained full functionality. They divided into two groups, with one team scaling the balcony on the south side and the other on the north. Aaron had been paired with Santero, Alderman and Dreyer.

Distant shouting and the footfalls of men running inside the house spoke to the effectiveness of Aaron's diversion, but he didn't stop until he reached the side yard, out of view of the backyard and the flames peeking over the rooftop from the burning truck. If he had to guess, he'd say the explosion had set the front of the house on fire, too. It had taken her days of meticulous engineering, but Camille had built a top-notch bomb.

He hoped she heard it and knew he'd come for her.

* * *

Camille stood over a semiconscious Two Down, whom she'd trussed with the curtain cord. Not that he'd be getting up anytime soon with the whack to the head she'd doled out. Staring down the barrel of Two Down's gun, she allowed herself a small grin of triumph until, over the blare of the television, she heard Rosalia whimper from behind the sofa.

Sadness swept through Camille as she thought of all the violent acts the little girl had witnessed. By incapacitating Two Down in front of Rosalia, she'd added to her terrible memories. But Camille couldn't think of any alternative ways to get them out of the house safely.

A rumble like a powerful earthquake shook the house. The air grew thick with smoke, as though the house was on fire. Bits of drywall crumbled from the wall. Books tumbled from shelves. Camille dived over Rosalia, shielding the little girl's trembling body with her own. "It's okay, sweetie. I've got you."

She held tight to Rosalia, and though it seemed improbable, a tendril of hope flared to life. Could it be that Aaron had come for them?

Men's voices hollered from the second floor along with the sounds of people running, reacting, assessing the damage. Camille pressed into the back of the sofa as two men darted through the room, shouting in Spanish.

"What were those men saying?" Camille asked in a whisper.

Rosalia looked at her with frightened eyes. "I don't know. Something about a Mérida cartel. Something bad. I want my mommy."

La Mérida Cartel? Camille blinked, wrapping her mind around a new possibility. Maybe Aaron and his ICE unit weren't responsible for the explosion and the house was under attack from a whole new enemy. Maybe Rosalia and Camille had landed in the middle of a war between two rival crime families.

"Time to go, sweetie. Give me your hand."

Rosalia shook her head but otherwise didn't budge.

Camille grabbed a lamp and ran to the window. Beyond the yard, three boats sat tied to a dock. Maybe one of them had keys in its ignition.

She heaved the lamp through the window, then swept Rosalia into her arms and ran.

Aaron, Dreyer, Alderman and Santero shot grappling hooks onto the balcony and yanked the scaling ropes to set the hooks against the wrought-iron rail. Given his experience as a rock climber, Aaron reached the balcony ledge first. The sliding glass door was closed, and the room beyond was dark and curtained. He ungracefully threw himself over the rail and onto the floor. The others followed.

They pulled their rifles around from their backs. These weren't M16s like Aaron had used before, but M4 Carbine semiautomatics designed not to choke up after an ocean swim. He loved the way the instrument felt in his hands, solid and precise and deadly.

Santero unhooked a stun grenade from his utility belt. Aaron had protested the plan to use a stun grenade until Dreyer assured him they were used all the time in combat when civilians were present. The flash and bang temporarily disoriented people inside the blasting range but didn't cause any pain or permanent damage. While Aaron hated the idea of Camille and Rosalia being within a blasting range of any kind, to get them out of Milán and Perez's grasp safely, he'd agreed to the grenade use.

Dreyer shattered the glass from the door with the butt of his rifle.

"Hooyah," Santero shouted. He plucked the pin out and shoved the grenade through the hole.

An earsplitting bang and bright flash lit up the room beyond. Aaron heard a similar boom from the balcony on the north side. Both teams breached the house simultaneously.

A man wearing blue pinstriped pajamas staggered toward the hallway door on the opposite side of the room.

"Freeze," Santero boomed.

Dreyer and Alderman rushed the guy and slammed him to the wall. Aaron held position at the hall door and heard the snap of cuffs being applied.

"Look familiar?" Santero asked.

"Milán," Dreyer answered.

Well, well. The big man himself.

Grabbing hold of Milán's shirt, Dreyer shook him hard. "Where are they, the woman and the girl you kidnapped?"

"Screw you."

Santero edged toward the door. "We don't have time for this. Alderman, lock him to the bathroom plumbing while we clear the building and search for Fisher—"

He stopped talking at the sound of footsteps in the hallway. Aaron aimed his M4 at the door as it opened.

Rodrigo Perez stood in the hall, barefoot and

shirtless. Black tattoos wrapped around his neck and down his torso and arms like a spreading fungus. A single scar sliced through the cleft of his chin. His bloodshot eyes zeroed in on Aaron. "You," he growled.

Aaron squeezed the trigger.

Like a frightened rabbit, Perez turned tail and took off.

Aaron squeezed off another round, then sprinted after him.

The world around him fell away. His breathing was even, his mind calm. No way was this rabbit going to disappear down a hole and escape. Perez had a head start and knowledge of the house's layout, but there was infinite power in being the man in pursuit instead of the one running for his life.

With each footfall through the hallway, then down a spiral staircase, Aaron felt his control of the situation hardening like steel in his spine. He tasted vengeance on his tongue, tasted his anticipation of the moment he overpowered Perez. Every horror Aaron and Camille had gone through in Mexico traced back to this man. The hurt, the fear, the constant struggle for survival—all because of Perez.

At the bottom of the stairs, Perez veered right across a living room with a blaring television and through a swinging door. Aaron trailed, shouldering through the door and into the kitchen. Perez skidded to a stop in front of a knife block on the far side of a rectangular island.

Aaron hit the island, leaned into it and fired. The shot pierced Perez's shoulder. With a grunt, Perez swung around and threw a knife in Aaron's direction.

Aaron ducked.

Adrenaline must have numbed Perez's pain because he seized the opportunity to bolt from the kitchen, a long-handled knife in his hand.

Aaron fired a round in his direction. He pushed through the door and ran across the living room in time to see Perez disappear out the back of the house through a broken window, the knife flashing in his hand. What an odd weapon of choice.

Surely the man had an arsenal of firepower at his disposal, so why a knife?

Santero and Dreyer caught up with him. "Wells and his team secured the basement. No sign of Fisher and the girl, but they found evidence that they might be on the property. They're searching the rest of the house."

Aaron gritted his teeth. *Come on, Camille. Where are you?*

One thing at a time. For now, he had a rabbit to catch. He snapped a fresh magazine into his gun. "Perez jumped out the window. But he's not going to get very far."

"We've got your back," Dreyer said, running behind him.

They leaped from the house to see Perez had made it as far as the dock.

"The bastard better not have a key to one of those boats," Santero muttered, squeezing off a handful of rounds.

Perez leaped onto the deck of the yacht and disappeared from view.

"Cover me," Aaron said, running.

The yacht's cabin door opened. Perez must've been crawling because Aaron couldn't see anybody. He cleared the rail of the boat and nosed his gun around the doorframe. "Nowhere to go from here, Perez. Come out with your hands above your head."

"Think again," said Perez from inside the cabin.

Santero and Dreyer moved into position on either side of the door. Santero pulled another stun grenade from his belt and handed it to Aaron. With a signal, Santero kicked the door open and Aaron tossed the grenade in.

Flash. Boom.

Aaron rushed in. Dreyer flicked on the light.

Perez stood amid the smoke near the stateroom door, his eyes watery and blinking, a sneer on his lips. His knife rested across Camille's throat.

Chapter 17

Aaron held himself in check but his entire body quivered with fury and dread. He visualized capping Perez in the forehead, but he couldn't take the chance of hitting Camille or Rosalia, who huddled under the table. Three assault rifles against one knife were great odds, except that Perez had to already know he was going down, so threatening his life with their guns was useless. Unless another variable entered the equation, their strategy boiled down to reaction time and opportunity.

Like the day they were kidnapped, Aaron met Camille's gaze with a look of fear that she countered with one of iron-willed determination. She gave him an almost imperceptible nod of warning.

"Aaron, I'm okay. He threatened Rosalia. I had to do something. Get her out of here."

Santero slid into line with Aaron, his rifle trained on Perez, too. "Dreyer, that's all you. Take the girl to the chopper."

Perez rattled the knife against Camille's throat. A trickle of blood dripped onto her shirt. "Rosalia belongs with me, her father. I can give her more than her *puta* of a mother, living in a roach-infested apartment. With me, she's part of Mexico's royalty, with the money and privilege that comes with my power."

Aaron forced his gaze from Camille to Perez's knife hand. It was suddenly clear why Perez wore gloves and why a knife was his weapon of choice.

El Ocho. What a fitting moniker. Rodrigo Perez had no thumbs.

Dreyer waited for Perez to finish his tirade, then crouched. "Come on, Rosalia. I'm going to take you back to California. Your mom's waiting for you there. She misses you."

"Get behind me, *mija*," Perez bit out. "Don't listen to these strangers. Listen to your papa."

Rosalia covered her ears and wailed louder. "I'm scared."

"I know you're scared, sweetie," Camille said. "But remember what I told you? I'm going to take you to your mama. You have to trust me. Go with Agent Dreyer."

"No, *mija.* They're lying to you. All of them."

After a long, soulful look at her father, Rosalia crawled into Dreyer's arms. "I want my mommy."

Cooing words of comfort, Dreyer whisked her from the room.

Fearing Perez's fury at his daughter's choice, Aaron took a step nearer, training his sights on Perez's elbow. "Stop moving that knife, Perez, or I'm going to move it for you."

Camille's hand flexed, catching Aaron's attention. Then her thumb retracted, as if she was counting down from five.

Whatever plan she's cooking up, she'd better not get herself killed.

Next to Aaron, Santero adjusted the grip on his rifle, his gaze on Camille's hand same as Aaron's was.

Three…two…one…

In a blur of movement, she grabbed the wrist of Perez's knife hand and locked her other hand around his elbow, seizing control of his arm and knife. She ducked under the elbow she held and pivoted, thrusting his wrist at his gut, stabbing him. As Aaron and Santero rushed forward, Perez released the knife with a howl of pain.

Camille twisted it farther in, then kicked him in the groin. He staggered, pulling the knife from his body.

Shouting a warning, Aaron lunged for her. She ducked and the knife sailed over her head.

Santero squeezed a round off and hit Perez between the eyes. He stumbled backward through the stateroom door and crumpled to the ground.

Aaron fell as the knife connected with his chest.

Pain blossomed from his torso to his limbs. He fought to keep his eyes focused and his breathing even.

"Aaron!" Camille knelt next to him. She ripped the wet-suit material from the wound site.

"Hurts. Is it deep?"

"No. Looks like the wet suit stopped it."

He angled his head and saw she was right. The knife had penetrated only about a half inch into his skin, hindered by the thick material and the zipper. He gnashed his teeth together and yanked it out with a grunt. Camille pressed a towel to his chest to staunch the blood flow.

"Camille," he said. "I have to tell you something."

"What is it?"

He took her hand. "I am sick and tired of people trying to kill you. It's getting on my nerves."

She let out a half laugh, half cry. "You're not the only one. How about we don't let it happen again?"

"Deal."

Santero wandered over from his inspection of Perez's body. He toed Aaron's foot. "Hey, you sure this broad needed us to rescue her? She seemed to be doing a bang-up job on her own."

Aaron smiled through the pain. "Knowing Camille, she would've been just fine without us."

"You know that's not true," she said quietly.

He winked.

Santero cleared his throat. "So, Fisher—Camille—those were quite the moves you put to that scumbag. Impressive. And totally hot. I've got to stay in Mexico to take care of this Vega cartel family Montgomery gave us a lead on, but how about next time I'm in the States I take you to dinner?"

Nice try, pal. Cringing in discomfort, Aaron pushed himself up and stood nose-to-nose with Santero.

"What?" Santero said. "I don't see you staking a claim on her."

"Staking a claim on me?" Camille spluttered.

"I got this, babe." Aaron wound back and

slammed his fist into Santero's jaw…and it was as sweet as he'd imagined. "You're a chauvinistic jackass, Santero. No woman likes to be treated like a piece of meat. You ought to learn some respect."

Santero rubbed his chin and regarded Aaron with a look of grudging admiration. "Guess that settles that." He nodded toward the door. "Choppers are out front. Let's roll."

The morning after their chopper flight to a Navy vessel in the international waters of the Pacific, Aaron found Camille sitting on deck, staring at the line of the horizon over the ocean with stormy eyes. His favorite worry wrinkle slashed a deep line between her eyebrows and her fidgety fingers twisted the bottom hem of her shirt.

He'd come to talk with her about their future, to help her realize that she loved him as much as he loved her, but clearly she already had some heavy stuff on her mind.

She spared Aaron only a glance as he sat beside her.

"I'm going to quit my job on the police force."

He cradled her hand in his. "Good."

"I'm not sure what my next career will be, but I wasn't meant to be cooped up behind a desk."

"No, you weren't."

"I'm going to take your advice and start over, build a new life for myself. A happy life. I want to get my passport and see the world."

Sounded great to him. He didn't think Dreyer would have any qualms about granting Aaron a nice, long vacation before he started his new position as an ICE agent. "Where do you want to travel first?"

She shrugged. "Maybe I'll just pick a direction and go."

Aaron pulled his face back. He was missing something. "You mean *we.*"

"Excuse me?"

"*We'll* pick a direction and go."

"Oh, Aaron, no." Her voice was heavy with

sadness. "You don't have to act like you want something more from me. I knew all along it was temporary."

What the hell was she trying to say? "What, exactly, do you think is going to happen between us once we get to San Diego?"

She looked distraught. "You know what'll happen. You'll get on with your life and I'll get on with mine." She hesitated, then pressed on. "If you're insinuating that you'd like to keep the option open for an occasional fling, then I'm sorry. I don't think I have it in me to be friends with benefits, or whatever it's called these days."

"Friends with benefits?" Now he was insulted. He pulled his face back. "You think I want us to be friends with benefits?"

"You're right. Of course you don't." Her eyes brimmed with moisture she tried to hide by turning her back to him.

The tears were like a slap to Aaron's face. His anger evaporated. "This whole time, you thought I was going to leave you the first chance I got?"

"You will. Monogamy's not your gig, remember? And anyway, I'd never pressure you. You have to know that. Even if it turns out I'm pregnant, you don't have to worry. I won't ask you for anything."

"What?"

Her outrageous assessment of the situation took his breath away. If he didn't know her so well, he'd be insulted. But know her, he did. He should have guessed that instead of trying to convince her she was in love with him, it was going to be the other way around for Little Miss Martyr.

He took her head in his hands and forced her to meet his eyes. "Camille, I could no more walk away from you than I could walk away from myself."

The twisting of her shirt grew more agitated.

"Talk to me."

Tears spilled over her cheeks. "You are a wonderful man, the best I've ever met. You shouldn't settle for someone less than perfect—someone who's broken."

"Broken?"

"My leg…"

Aaron shook his head at her flimsy logic. "I think I can work around a five-year-old gunshot wound."

"Post-traumatic stress disorder. My hand shakes."

"Unless you're worried you won't be able to shoot me should you get it in your mind to, I hardly see how that matters." He grinned in an effort to coax her to do the same, but she wasn't having any of it.

"You could have any woman you want."

"Damn right I can. I do, right here. What's the real problem, Camille?"

She screwed her lips up. "I can't make you happy. If you settled for me because you were trying to do the right thing, you'd grow to resent me."

"Don't I get to decide what makes me happy?"

"Yes, but—"

"So if I say the idea of spending the rest of my

life with you makes me happy, are you going to tell me I'm wrong?"

"But—"

He put a finger to her lips. "Hear me out, okay? You and me, we belong together. All that eternal bachelor stuff I used to think I wanted? I was so stupid. I had no idea how perfect and wonderful it felt to really love someone the way I love you."

"You love me?"

Stubborn woman. "More than I ever thought it was possible to love another human being."

"You love me?" Camille sat as though frozen, her eyes glazed over, weighing this new information. "Why didn't you tell me so sooner?"

Aaron chuckled, relieved she believed him, and hauled her onto his lap. "I didn't want to scare you away. Please say you'll let me take care of you for the rest of your life. Please tell me you can love me back."

She smiled and stroked his jaw. Good. They were getting somewhere.

"These past two years, I wrote off my feelings

for you as physical attraction," she said. "But that night in the ferry, after we planted the bomb, I couldn't deny it anymore. I realized I loved you, but I thought it would take a miracle for you to have feelings for me."

He scoffed. "It wasn't a miracle. It was inevitable. The first time I saw you kicking some serious cartel ass, I was a goner."

"Aaron, are you sure about this? I don't think I'd survive if you changed your mind."

He'd never been more sure of anything in his life. "Don't be so afraid, my proud warrior. I'm not going to hurt you." He poured his love into a tender kiss.

Four days later, the water of the San Diego bay glittered in the afternoon sun as the Navy vessel docked. The journey home had been uneventful. Two days into their trip, word came from ICE headquarters that Santero and his team had delivered five members of the Vega family to Mexican authorities, including Ana and Ramón. They faced a laundry list of charges in their own country, as well as extradition to the United States.

While a piece of Aaron halfheartedly wished he could've assisted in the Vega family's capture, all he really wanted to do for the time being was lay low with Camille—and maybe, if luck was on his side, the baby they'd created.

After a first emotional night, Rosalia had settled into the idea that she was returning home. Camille's own mothering instincts had taken over and she had doted on her new charge with calm self-assurance. On the phone with her boss, she'd lobbied hard for a discreet reunion between Rosalia and her mother, but Aaron had a feeling that was impossible. Rosalia's kidnapping and rescue was far too sensational a story to be ignored by the ravenous American press.

After much debate, Aaron and Camille alerted Jacob and Juliana to their arrival, but not their parents. Camille, who especially hated being the center of attention, wanted only to hand Rosalia off to her mother, meet Jacob and Juliana's new baby and drop off the grid for a while. They owed ICE and the police innumerable hours of debriefing, but certainly they were entitled to some downtime after spending weeks on the run.

Two unmarked police cars, an ambulance and at least a dozen people met them at the marina. A woman with auburn hair and a stout build pushed through the crowd and reached the boat first.

"Mama!" Rosalia shouted with glee.

Camille lifted her over the edge. They watched as mother and daughter cried and embraced.

Aaron scanned the crowd for Jacob and found him standing in the shade with the petite brunette who had captured his heart. Juliana was clutching a pink bundle in her arms.

Jacob looked content, if not a little worn-out, standing with his wife and child. Juliana looked very little like Camille, who had at least three inches on her younger sibling and was far more voluptuous. Both shared the same nose and green eyes, but it was easy to see how Camille had settled into the role of the protective, take-charge big sister.

He squeezed Camille's hand. "Ready?"

"Ready." She took a breath, squared her shoulders and marched from the dock.

Aaron followed, marveling at her. She radiated self-efficiency and unflagging strength, but he knew better. He was keenly aware of the privilege it was to be the only man allowed to see her at her most vulnerable and he loved her all the more for it.

Camille and Juliana reached each other first, embracing and cooing over the baby. Aaron and Jacob hugged and slapped each other's backs. Then the teasing began.

"Is that a perm you've got, bro?" Jacob asked. "And brown, too? I've never seen your hair that dark and shaggy before."

"Hell, I thought it was Halloween with those dark circles you've got under your eyes. You put makeup on to get them that way or did you give up on sleeping?"

Jacob wiped a hand over his face. "I tell you what, this parenting stuff really knocks it out of you. Just you wait. Someday you'll know what I mean."

Aaron smiled. They'd need a pregnancy test to confirm it, but in the past few days, the signs all pointed to the possibility that a new life had taken root the first time he and Camille made love.

Camille eased the little pink bundle from Juliana's arms into her own and stole away to a bench. "Hello, Alana Rose. I'm your aunt Camille."

Aaron watched her with a wistful smile. "Did you bring it?" he whispered to Jacob.

Jacob rummaged in his jacket and handed Aaron his car keys. "Brought your car, like you wanted, but something tells me this is what you're really asking about." He slipped a small black velvet box into Aaron's hand.

"That's what I meant. Thank you."

Jacob eyed him curiously. "Your mom was pretty suspicious when I asked for your grandmother's wedding ring. She made me promise to tell you to use it wisely."

Aaron grinned even wider. "No worries there."

"Are you sure about this? Last I heard, you two hated each other."

"Yeah, that was way too much work. This—" Aaron rattled the box "—is much easier than pretending to hate her ever was."

"I bet it is. Your mom would have liked to see you today, you know. She and your dad have been worried."

"We wanted as little fanfare as possible. And I was afraid once my mom got a hold of me, she might never let go. Pass it on to them that we'll be back soon. This is just something we have to do for a while."

At that moment, Juliana rushed by. "Camille, are you crying?"

Aaron's head snapped up to see Camille holding the baby with fat tears streaming down her cheeks. Jacob snagged Juliana's arm. "Let Aaron take care of her."

Juliana responded, but Aaron didn't hear what she said. He strode to Camille, scooped both her and the baby into his arms and sat on the bench. He spared a glance and a wink at a stunned Juliana, who stood frozen, gawking at them open-mouthed.

Between sniffles, Camille said dejectedly, "I'm crying, Aaron. I can't stop."

"It's okay to cry, babe."

"Not for me."

Aaron chuckled and tucked some stray hairs behind her ear. He'd loved her blond hair, but he'd take her any way she came. And the chocolate-brown was starting to grow on him. "It's been one heck of a ride." Then he whispered for her ears only, "Not to mention that your hormones are all out of whack."

Despite her tears, she deviously arched a brow at him. "My sister will strangle us for not telling her right away."

"She and my mom will have to fight each other for the honor. But you and I deserve a little time to enjoy the news privately. We've earned that much, I think."

"Yes, we have." She swiped at the wetness on her cheeks.

"Glad I found you both." It was one of the officers who'd escorted Rosalia's mom to the boat. "Sit tight because reporters are on the way. You're national heroes now. Your faces are going to be all over the news."

Aaron cringed. "Thanks for the warning." After the officer walked away, he kissed Camille's cheek. "I don't know about you, but being a national hero isn't on my agenda today."

"Uh, no."

"Then that's our cue to leave. Let me hold my goddaughter once before we go." He placed Camille on her feet and took the baby. "Hey, Alana, your aunt Camille and I are going to take off, so don't do anything interesting until we get back, okay? Take good care of your mommy and daddy for us."

With a kiss to her chubby, soft cheek, he handed her to Juliana, whose mouth still hung wide open.

He kissed the top of Juliana's head and punched Jacob on the shoulder. Then he offered Camille his hand. "Will you come with me, Camille?"

She crossed her arms and smiled indulgently at him. "Where to?"

He twirled his car keys. "Thought we'd just pick a direction and go."

That garnered a laugh from her as she entwined her fingers with his. Making her laugh was probably his favorite thing in the world. He planned to spend a lot of time in the future perfecting the art.

"How about north," she suggested. "I'm sure they've got great doctors in San Francisco."

"Doctors?" Juliana asked. "Why do you need a doctor? Are you hurt?"

Camille answered with a dismissive wave of her hand. "Don't worry about it."

Aaron caught a suspicious look from Jacob. He ignored it. "North it is."

Jacob shook his head, chuckling. "Have fun, you two."

Camille gave Juliana a one-armed hug. Juliana stammered and gestured at Aaron and Camille's joined hands. "When did you and Aaron…um… You look happy, Cam. You're glowing."

"I'll tell you about it soon, but we need to hit the road before the news vans show up."

Aaron smiled at her. "Ready to ride off into the sunset, babe?"

"Ready." Camille gave Jacob a quick hug, then walked with Aaron toward the parking lot.

"Not sure how you'd feel about the idea, but I've got the sudden urge to buy a boat."

Camille laughed. "Funny you should mention it. Me, too."

"You know, *Blondie* would make a terrific boat name."

She shook her head. "It would, but I think we should name it after the boat we fell in love on. What did you say before—it pretty much sums up our whole experience in Mexico?"

"At the time, I was being sarcastic."

"True, but *Happily Ever After* isn't such a big joke to me anymore. In fact, I'd say it's just about perfect."

* * * * *

1	2	3	4	5	6	7	8	9	10	11	12	13	14	15
16	17	18	19	20	21	22	23	24	25	26	27	28	29	30
31	32	33	34	35	36	37	38	39	40	41	42	43	44	45
46	47	48	49	50	51	52	53	54	55	56	57	58	59	60
61	62	63	64	65	66	67	68	69	70	71	72	73	74	75
76	77	78	79	80	81	82	83	84	85	86	87	88	89	90
91	92	93	94	95	96	97	98	99	100					

101	102	103	104	105	106	107	108	109	110	111	112	113	114	115
116	117	118	119	120	121	122	123	124	125	126	127	128	129	130
131	132	133	134	135	136	137	138	139	140	141	142	143	144	145
146	147	148	149	150	151	152	153	154	155	156	157	158	159	160
161	162	163	164	165	166	167	168	169	170	171	172	173	174	175
176	177	178	179	180	181	182	183	184	185	186	187	188	189	190
191	192	193	194	195	196	197	198	199	200					

201	202	203	204	205	206	207	208	209	210	211	212	213	214	215
216	217	218	219	220	221	222	223	224	225	226	227	228	229	230
231	232	233	234	235	236	237	238	239	240	241	242	243	244	245
246	247	248	249	250	251	252	253	254	255	256	257	258	259	260
261	262	263	264	265	266	267	268	269	270	271	272	273	274	275
276	277	278	279	280	281	282	283	284	285	286	287	288	289	290
291	292	293	294	295	296	297	298	299	300					

301	302	303	304	305	306	307	308	309	310	311	312	313	314	315
316	317	318	319	320	321	322	323	324	325	326	327	328	329	330
331	332	333	334	335	336	337	338	339	340	341	342	343	344	345
346	347	348	349	350	351	352	353	354	355	356	357	358	359	360
361	362	363	364	365	366	367	368	369	370	371	372	373	374	375
376	377	378	379	380	381	382	383	384	385	386	387	388	389	390
391	392	393	394	395	396	397	398	399	400					

401	402	403	404	405	406	407	408	409	410	411	412	413	414	415
416	417	418	419	420	421	422	423	424	425	426	427	428	429	430
431	432	433	434	435	436	437	438	439	440	441	442	443	444	445
446	447	448	449	450	451	452	453	454	455	456	457	458	459	460
461	462	463	464	465	466	467	468	469	470	471	472	473	474	475
476	477	478	479	480	481	482	483	484	485	486	487	488	489	490
491	492	493	494	495	496	497	498	499	500					

M/c 3209

876	877	878	879	880	881	882	883	884	885	886	887	888	889	890
891	892	893	894	895	896	897	898	899	900					

901	902	903	904	905	906	907	908	909	910	911	912	913	914	915
916	917	918	919	920	921	922	923	924	925	926	927	928	929	930
931	932	933	934	935	936	937	938	939	940	941	942	943	944	945
946	947	948	949	950	951	952	953	954	955	956	957	958	959	960
961	962	963	964	965	966	967	968	969	970	971	972	973	974	975
976	977	978	979	980	981	982	983	984	985	986	987	988	989	990
991	992	993	994	995	996	997	998	999	1000					

M/c 3318

C0000 009 340 839